COOL BEANS

COOL BEANS
THE FURTHER ADVENTURES OF BEANBOY

by

LISA HARKRALER

HOUGHTON MIFFLIN HARCOURT
Boston   New York

For information about permission to reproduce selections
from this book, write to trade.permissions@hmhco.com or to
Permissions, Houghton Mifflin Harcourt Publishing Company,
3 Park Avenue, 19th Floor, New York, New York 10016.

www.hmhco.com

The text of this book is set in Caecilia.

The illustrations are digital.
The Library of Congress has cataloged the hardcover
edition as follows:
Harkrader, Lisa.
Cool Beans : the further adventures of Beanboy / by Lisa
Harkrader.
p. cm.
Summary: "This sequel to *The Adventures of Beanboy* com-
bines comic illustrations, a small-town bully facing off
against a budding artist, and a rousing, decisive game of
dodgeball." —Provided by publisher
[1. Bullying—Fiction. 2. Comic books, strips, etc.—Fiction. 3.
Middle schools—Fiction. 4. Schools—Fiction. 5. Brothers—Fiction.] I. Title.
PZ7.H22615Coo 2014
[Fic]—dc23
2013032667

ISBN: 978-0-544-03904-9 hardcover
ISBN: 978-0-544-54069-9 paperback

Manufactured in the United States of America
7 2021
4500822997

For my editor, Ann Rider, who, with superhuman patience and stealth, nudges me to make each book better before I even realize what she's doing.

And for my dad, Robert Knudsen, my own personal superhero and the best person I know.

one

I dragged the door open. The bell jingled against the glass, and a swell of warm sporting-goods air bulged out to greet us.

Beecher pushed past me into the brightly lit store. I followed and we stood side by side, wiping our sneakers on the big mat inside the door and giving our noses a chance to thaw out.

"Oooo." Beech squinted over the top of his fogged-up glasses. "Tool."

My brother has a problem with c's. They come out sounding like t's.

I pulled off his glasses, wiped the fog on the hood of his coat, and slid the glasses back on his face.

"Ooooooo!" He blinked as the blur of shine and color suddenly sharpened into racks of jerseys and shoes. "*Really* tool."

He stood there, barely breathing, taking it all in. The bats. The balls. The tables heaped with Wheaton University hoodies. The giant flat screens mounted high in the corners, all tuned to the same basketball game, the play-by-play blasting through the store.

We'd been here before, lots of times, back when Dad still lived with us, before he moved to Boston. Beech had been pretty little then, so he probably didn't remember. Still, he'd never been a sporty kid, so who knows why soccer cleats were suddenly so fascinating to him.

"Superhero tore," he said, his voice filled with wonder.

I looked at him. "What?"

"Superhero. Tore." He threw his mittened hands wide. "See?"

"I see sports equipment," I said.

Beech gave me a sad look and shook his head,

2

like I was a pitiful case if I couldn't recognize a superhero store when I was standing in one.

And really, as I unzipped my coat and peeled off
my gloves, I realized he was kind of right.

- Stretchy high-tech jersey

- Scientifically advanced
  baseball bat

- Bulging muscles

- Stretchy high-tech
  superhero uniform

- Scientifically advanced
  goggles and utility belt

- Bulging muscles

One difference: No capes in sports. Except maybe
pro wrestling.

I headed toward a rack of high-tech workout shirts. Here in Wheaton, Kansas, I was not known as a superior athlete (or, well, any kind of athlete). Still, I could totally rock a shirt like that. Comic book geniuses may not be ripped, but we get sweaty too.

I whisked through the hangers on the rack, thinking black might be my speed. Or no—red, like Spider-Man. *And* like the Red Sox. (My dad would like the Red Sox part.)

I stopped. Dad was going to ask me what I bought. He was going to flat out ask. I couldn't tell him T-shirts. I wouldn't be able to stand the disappointment crackling through the phone line.

Beech tugged on the bottom of my coat. "Tut." It was his way of saying my name. "Ine Man."

"Beech. This is a sports store. There's no Iron Man."

"Uh-*huh*." Beech whipped off his mittens, shoved them at me, and shot like a laser to the baseball aisle, the hood of his puffy winter coat flopping against his back.

I caught up with him beside a display of baseball helmets.

He stood on tiptoe, inching his stubby fingers toward a helmet at the top.

"Ine Man." His voice was hushed with awe.

"Beech. It's a baseball helmet."

I pulled it down and handed it to him.

He held it like a precious jewel. "Ine Man."

And in a weird way—again—he was kind of right.

Beech lifted the helmet and placed it reverently

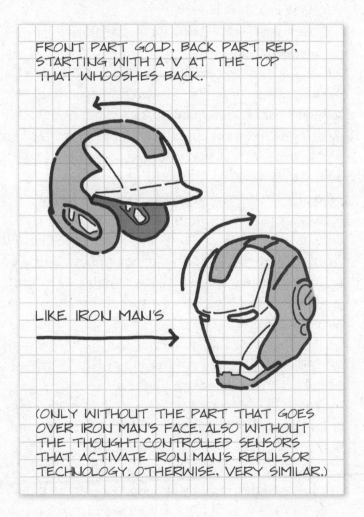

FRONT PART GOLD, BACK PART RED, STARTING WITH A V AT THE TOP THAT WHOOSHES BACK.

LIKE IRON MAN'S

(ONLY WITHOUT THE PART THAT GOES OVER IRON MAN'S FACE. ALSO WITHOUT THE THOUGHT-CONTROLLED SENSORS THAT ACTIVATE IRON MAN'S REPULSOR TECHNOLOGY. OTHERWISE, VERY SIMILAR.)

on his head, as if he were crowning himself king. It dropped down over his eyes. He tipped his head back so he could peer out at me.

"Tool?" he said.

"Way cool," I said.

"Hey, guys. Can I help you find anything?"

I looked up.

A girl in a Bottenfield's T-shirt stood beside us, flashing a sporty smile. The white plastic name tag pinned to her shirt said JESSICA, and I could tell right away she was big into athletics. Her hair was pulled back in that perky sort of ponytail girls wear when they play sports, with shiny blond streaks, probably from playing outdoor sports, and her high-performance running shoes gave her a sporty bounce when she walked. You could tell she felt right at home around athletic equipment. She even had a neon pink soccer ball tucked under her arm.

"I don't think so," I said. "We're not sure what we're looking for."

Beech nodded. The helmet slid down over his face. His voice echoed out from under it: "Tarts."

"Tarts?" Jessica looked confused.

I deciphered for her. "Cards," I said. "Gift cards. From our dad. For Christmas. We're here to spend them."

"Ah." She nodded. Her ponytail bounced. "I get it. Just look around, and if you need help, let me know."

6

She started to turn away.

"Tut superhero," the helmet told her.

Jessica stopped.

I closed my eyes.

We'd been through this with our downstairs neighbors, two different breakfast waitresses at the Atomic Flapjack, and the guy who emptied the change machine at the laundromat. And even though it was nice that my goober of a brother thought I was a superhero, I knew in my heart it would only end up one way: me looking pathetic.

Jessica smiled down at Beech, in that bright way people smile when they're trying to figure out what he's saying. "You?" she asked him. "You're a superhero?"

"No." Beech tipped the helmet back. "Tut." He grabbed the front of my shirt and tugged.

She gave him another bright smile. "Tut?"

"He means Tuck." I peeled his fingers from my shirt. "Short for Tucker. It's what he calls me."

"Tut draw superhero. And win." Beecher threw his hands wide. "Win *big*."

Jessica looked at me.

I shrugged, kind of embarrassed because I didn't want to brag. And also because it was a pretty big deal and I kind of *did* want to brag.

"You know H2O?" I said.

"Big superhero," said Beech. "Really tool."

Jessica nodded, clearly puzzled.

"They had this contest to invent a sidekick for him. I invented a sidekick named Beanboy and sort of"—another shrug—"won."

"Oh!" Jessica's confusion cleared up. "Just like my niece. She won first prize in the art contest at her grade school."

"Yeah," I said, even though it wasn't like that at all.

Jessica flashed another smile. "You guys let me know if you need any help, okay?"

She ambled off in her bouncy white running shoes, and as she went, she gave the pink soccer ball a spin and stuck her index finger under it.

I stayed where I was, looking pathetic.

Dad had told us to spend the two gift cards on anything we wanted. I'd tucked them in my shoe. The round plastic corners were starting to wear a blister on my foot.

Beech wanted a batting helmet. He wouldn't use it for actual batting, of course. But I knew for sure he'd sleep in the dang thing. So *he* was taken care of.

I left Beech admiring himself and the helmet in a mirror, and wandered through the aisles, searching for my sport.

I sighed. This would be a lot easier if Dad had sent gift cards to Caveman Comics. At Caveman, I wouldn't even have to look around. I'd head straight for the Reference Section, pull *The Dark Overlord Comics Encyclopedia: The Definitive Guide to the Dark Overlord Universe* from the top shelf, third book from the left, haul it to the counter, and plunk down my gift card. The whole thing would take approximately twelve seconds.

I ran my hand over a lacrosse stick. Because who knows? I could have a real gift for lacrosse.

Or no—fencing.

I slid a fencing foil from the rack. It was kind of like a light saber. Without the light part.

Fencing might be just the thing to bring out my inner Jedi. I wielded the foil before me in both hands and spun around, ready to take on the Empire. The bell jangled against the Bottenfield's door, and a clump of guys blasted in on a gust of late December air. Guys from my school. Guys who actually belonged in a sporting-goods store. One guy especially. Wesley Banks.

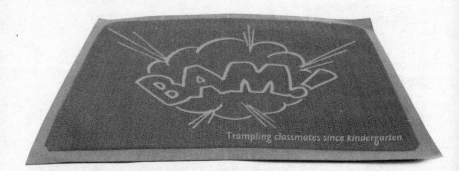

Trampling classmates since kindergarten

two

Wesley Banks wasn't by himself.

He was never by himself.

When he strode into Bottenfield's, shook the cold out of his hair, planted his feet wide on the mat inside the door, and flipped his black shades onto his head to scope out the scene, T.J. Hawkins and Luke Delgado strode, shook, planted, and flipped right behind him. The gunslinger and his gang. Butch and Sundance and another Sundance.

If athletes were superheroes, you'd have to call Wesley Banks the superhero of Amelia M. Earhart Middle School, maybe all of Wheaton, probably whole chunks of northeast Kansas.

Wesley Banks scored runs and baskets and touch-

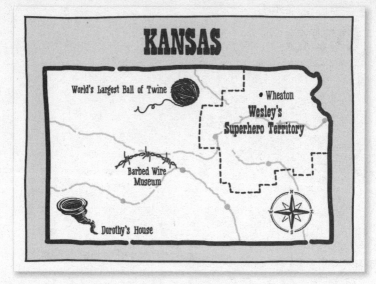

downs and goals. He sacked quarterbacks and turned double plays. He won games single-handedly. Didn't matter what he was playing. You could invent a whole new sport—upside-down water basket-bowling—and Wesley would be the star.

Wesley strode toward the aisles of sports equipment.

I quickly developed a plan:

1. Stop making the embarrassing hum/buzz light saber sound in my throat.
2. Stay crouched behind the rack of fencing swords till Wesley and his gunslingers were gone.

"NOOOOO!"

I closed my eyes. My plan had forgotten about Beech.

"NOOOOOOOO!" His screech echoed through Bottenfield's. "Ine Man. *Ine Man.*"

I peeked over the fencing display. I couldn't see him past all the shelves and displays. But I heard him.

"Mine! *Mine.*"

I slid my foil back onto the rack and wove my way through the aisles to the baseball section. I found him facing off against Butch and the Sundances. I flicked a glance at them. "What's going on, Beechman?"

His face was scrunched in pure panic, his body stiff. He pointed a trembling finger at Wesley, who was now holding the red and gold batting helmet.

"Ine Man," Beech said. His voice trembled, too.

Wesley gave a shrug. "Don't have a clue what he's saying."

He tossed the helmet from one mighty hand to the other. He'd had an early growth spurt, back when we were still in grade school, and now he loomed over me, with his big shoulders and all his muscles.

He kept his gaze steady, daring me to challenge him.

I swallowed. I wasn't a gunslinger. I didn't have a gang. No Butches. No Sundances. No muscle tone to speak of.

I steeled myself, steeled my bony shoulders under my big winter coat. "My brother's going to buy that helmet," I told Wesley. "That's what he's saying."

"Sorry," said Wesley, "but it's mine. I picked it up. I'm buying it."

"You picked it up off his head."

Wesley shrugged. "Finders keepers. Losers . . . well, that would be you and the little dork."

He aimed a laugh at the Sundances, who nervously laughed back.

I clenched my fists. "He's not a dork. He's a little kid, and he had it first."

"Right." Wesley laughed again. "Like *he* needs a batting helmet."

I clenched harder. I could feel my fingernails digging into the palms of my hands.

"Give it back to him," I said.

"Or what?"

"Give it back to him."

Wesley stared at me. Stared me down cold, his eyes not flinching. "Why? It's not like he's ever going to play baseball."

I stared back. Tried not to flinch, even though I know I did.

"How do *you* know?"

Wesley gave a snort. "Look at him."

I didn't have to look at him. I'd been looking at him for nine years, and I knew exactly what he looked like. At this very moment he was white and shaky and about to pass out from rage and frustration and helplessness and flat-out fear.

"He's going to play baseball," I said.

Another snort. "Right."

"No! No baseball." Beech grabbed my arm. Panic shot through his voice. "Superhero. *Superhero.*"

I closed my eyes. *Thanks, Beech.*

Wesley looked at him. His mouth twisted into a smile. Not a friendly, sporty smile, like Jessica's. Not a superhero's smile. Not a smile with a speck of happiness in it.

15

A slow, mean, hard smile.

"Superhero?" Wesley put the helmet on his head. He turned to model it for Luke and T.J. "Look at me," he said. "I'm a superhero."

He held out his arms, I guess to act like he was flying, and flapped them this way and that.

Wesley Banks might have been the greatest athlete to ever step onto a Wheaton, Kansas, ball field, but he didn't have the first clue about superheroes.

"Tut!" Beech clamped his fingers onto my arm. They dug into my coat sleeve. "*Tut!*"

Wesley stopped. Stared at me, his eyes wide, his hard smile even wider. "Tut? Is that your superhero name? *Tut?*"

He cut a look at Luke and T.J., and all three of them laughed.

"Well, *Tut*. This helmet's mine." Wesley tucked it under his arm. "So I guess you'll have to find another one just like it. Except, oops! You can't. This is the last one."

He fired off one more hard, smirky smile, then pushed past us toward the cash register. Luke and T.J. followed.

"Tut!" Beech stared after them in horror.

"I know," I said. "I got it."

I bent over and dug inside my shoe for the gift cards. They'd worked themselves down my sock and lodged under my heel. I ripped my shoe off.

The bell jingled against the door, and another blast of winter air swept through Bottenfield's. Swept down the aisles, rattling the hangers of jerseys and baseball pants and fluttering the FENCING sign tacked over the rack of foils. Swept over me and Beech and ruffled my hair back from my face.

I looked up—

—straight into the eyes of Emma Quinn, shiniest girl in all of Wheaton.

The morning sun shone behind her, so that standing there in the doorway of Bottenfield's—her cheeks glowing pink from the cold, her eyelashes sparkling with snow, the fur-lined hood of her winter coat pushed back from her shiny blond hair— she fairly shimmered. Like she'd been sprinkled with fairy dust. I think maybe the Kaleys were with her—they usually were—but I couldn't see them. I couldn't see anything but Emma. And all that fairy dust.

She waved a gloved hand at me. "Hey, Tuck," she said, and even her voice glistened.

I crouched there, frozen, my shoe tucked under my arm, my hand still jammed into my sock. My body was paralyzed, my tongue twisted around my tonsils.

"I—uh—erg," I finally managed to say back.

It wasn't my fault. Emma Quinn possessed the most powerful superpower in all of Wheaton: the superhuman ability to jam all signals to and from a person's mind, rendering their brain cells completely useless.

The cash register binged.

Emma swept her glistening gaze toward the front counter.

"Oh, hey, Wesley," she said.

Wesley gave her a casual tip of his chin. "Hey."

The register churned and spit out a receipt, and before I could do a thing about it, Jessica slipped the receipt into a plastic sack along with the helmet.

Wesley snatched it up and turned toward the door.

"See ya, *Tut*," he said as he blew past, out the door and into the cold, the Bottenfield's bag swinging from his wrist.

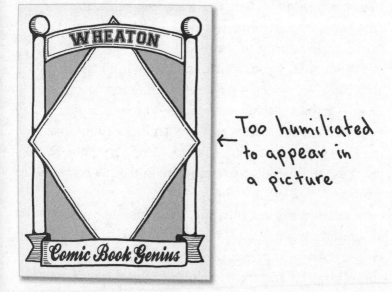

Too humiliated
to appear in
a picture

three

I stomped into the Batcave, a.k.a. my bedroom, and chucked my coat onto the bed. I paced the creaky floorboards in front of my desk.

What was wrong with me? I couldn't even go shopping—*shopping*—without turning into a big fat loser—*in front of the shiniest girl in Wheaton, Kansas.*

I strode back toward my bed. Thought about kicking my desk chair, but that would only bring my mom down the hall, determined to find out what was wrong.

I heaved myself into my chair instead. A sheet of smooth, white Bristol board stared up at me. Mrs. Frazee had asked everyone in Art Club to create something artistic for the club's bulletin board over winter break. I'd started sketching out a poster.

I didn't even want to look at it now.

But the drawing just sat there on my desk, staring at me. Before I knew what I was doing, I popped the cap off my permanent black marker and started inking in the details of Beanboy's stretchy crime-fighting costume.

It wasn't just a school art contest, no matter what Jessica or the Flapjack waitresses or the guy at the laundromat thought. It was a prestigious, *national* contest. I'd gotten the winning letter right before winter break, and ever since then, since that day, I'd felt like some kind of small-town superhero. A ruler-wielding superhero with a pencil grip of steel.

I'd strutted around my house feeling like a superhero. I hung with Noah at Caveman Comics feeling like a superhero (especially since the last time we trekked in there, Caveman himself had glanced up from his graphic novel and uttered two entire words—"Dude. Intense."—before burying his shaggy head in his novel again and completely ignoring me). I felt like I could be a superhero anywhere in Wheaton, anywhere in Kansas, anywhere in the *universe* (if, you know, I actually went places).

Marker Man   Sketcher X   Captain Artistic-O

And then I'd walked into Bottenfield's.

My marker squeaked as I blackened Beanboy's mask.

It was the classic dilemma. Superman: one kick-butt superhero. Alter ego, Clark Kent: nice guy, decent reporter, never going to kick anything, butt or otherwise.

Tucker MacBean, Comic Book Genius, felt like a superhero.

Tucker MacBean, Real Live Person? Not even close.

The afternoon sun flung its weak yellow rays against my second-floor window. The winter wind skittered over the glass, searching for a way in.

But the Batcave was my fortress, my watchtower, where nothing from the outside could touch me. As the tip of my marker glided over the smooth surface of the Bristol board, inking the perfect curve of Beanboy's cape, that superhero feeling washed over me again. The rest of the world fell away, till it was just me, my marker, and the Bristol board, pulling the comic book vision in my head onto the blank white paper on my desk.

I sat back in my chair and studied my drawing.

It was probably the same feeling baseball players get when they knock one over the fence. They know it's out of the park the instant they hit it, just from the feel of the impact, from the crack of the bat.

The difference was, comic book artists didn't have bleachers of fans leaping to their feet to cheer or mobs of teammates carrying them off the field on their shoulders.

I absently spun the marker between my fingers. It was something I'd done my whole life, whenever I was drawing. Between my fingers. Around my thumb. Mostly I never thought about it.

But I thought about it now. I thought about Jessica spinning the pink soccer ball. I thought about me spinning my marker. And I thought about how the world sees those two things. Spinning a ball—*amazing!* Spinning a pencil—lame.

But who made that rule? I mean it. Who decided that balls are cool and drawing pencils are boring? That muscles are impressive, but excellent manual dexterity (like mine), not so much? That ball players like Wesley Banks would be the all-star major leaguers of middle school, while comic book geniuses like me would forever ride the pine?

I capped my marker (carefully—it was a professional model my mom had given me for Christmas, and I didn't want it to dry out) and rummaged through my closet. I dug through shoes and old

Halloween costumes and my science fair project from fifth grade and finally wrestled out the basketball my dad had sent me two years ago.

I measured the heft of it between my hands. It was just a dang ball. I could spin it as well as anyone. I held my finger up, balanced the ball, and gave it a spin. It wobbled off, bounced across the floor, and banged into my desk chair.

"Tucker?" Mom's voice echoed down the hallway. "Is everything okay?"

"Fine," I hollered back.

"Good."

I waited for a minute. I was pretty sure she wasn't done.

I was right.

"Don't forget your resolution," she called out.

I sighed. Mom was big on New Year's resolutions. She called them a "once-a-year opportunity to become a better person and a more respectable human being." She made all three of us write down our resolutions.

I had to help Beech with his resolution, which was the same every year. He told me what to write and then he drew a picture so he'd remember what he'd said.

Mom always stuck our resolutions under magnets on the refrigerator so we could look at them for encouragement. (Beech didn't really need any more encouragement. He already practiced flying around the MacBean Family Apartment nonstop, his pillowcase cape flapping behind him, usually flapping his incredibly patient older brother in the face.)

And I have to admit, I usually liked our resolutions. It was something we did every year, a family

Beecher MacBean's
New Year's Resolution

Practice Superhero Flying so I
don't fall down so much.

BEECHEr

tradition, which the MacBeans were sorely in need of now that a major chunk of us—Dad—lived halfway across the country.

Plus, who doesn't want to be a more respectable human being?

But this year, even though it was almost New Year's Eve, I hadn't even *thought* about a resolution. I mean, hadn't I just won a (prestigious! national!) comic book contest? Resolution-wise, how do you top that?

I crawled under my desk to retrieve the basket-ball. I thought about trying to spin it again but shoved it back into my closet instead.

I definitely needed a resolution.

four

Noah and I squeaked down the empty hallway of Amelia M. Earhart Middle School, battered lockers standing at attention at either side, early January slush dripping from our sneakers. My bookbag banged along against my back. Noah's faithful companion—his bassoon case—banged along against his. It was our first day back from winter break, and I'd talked Noah into getting here early so he could help me.

Case File: The Spoonster

Status: Sidekick.

Base: Basically, the Earhart Middle School band room.

Superpower: Preventive action. (Noah always arrives early; always carries Kleenex; keeps four quarters, two spare pencils, an extra pair of gym shorts, and a tiny screwdriver—to fix his glasses and jimmy open my locker—in his bassoon case; and never leaves his homework till the last minute. Preventive action comes in handy more often than you'd think.)

Superweapon: His huge brain. (Noah is, like, the smartest kid ever. It's not his fault. His parents don't allow him to be stupid. They've enrolled him in every extracurricular activity invented, from music lessons to anthropology camp. Now he knows everything, including how to play ancient Korean folk tunes on the bassoon. Which goes over big in the seventh grade.)

Real Name: Noah Spooner

Now he held my first poster, reading.

I didn't want to look like I was watching him, so I acted fascinated by the flyers taped to the walls announcing sign-ups for the school carnival and the Last Player Standing tournament, plus marker-

drawn signs plastered all over the lockers, little cut-outs with peppy sayings like *Win!*, *Rebound!*, *Go, Kaley!*, *We're #1!*

"Excellent beginning," Noah said finally. "Let's see the others."

I stopped long enough to shuffle the first poster to the back and hand him the next. We squeaked along once more.

I flicked a covert look at Noah. Poster #2 was where things started to get good.

I kept acting all fascinated by the school hallway, even though it looked exactly the same as it always did. A little cleaner, probably, since the janitor had all of winter break to scrape up gunk from the floor. Plus outside the math room, somebody had tied a pair of sneakers together and tossed them over one of the fluorescent light fixtures on the ceiling. I felt sorry for whoever had thrown them up there. They'd be spending some quality time in Mr. Petrucelli's office soon.

Noah handed me poster #2. I handed him #3, the last one.

Noah handed me the last poster after reading it. "Extreme," he said.

I looked at him. "Really?"

He nodded and gave me an encouraging fist bump.

Wow. "Extreme" was Noah's best compliment. Usually only Mozart, Stan Lee, and whoever invented

the wireless game controller rated as extreme. And now Beanboy. This was big.

But would anybody else at Earhart Middle think so? Or even notice?

I straightened the posters into a neat stack and slipped them back into their all-weather watertight carrying case (a.k.a. the trash bag I had swiped from our kitchen cupboard).

Noah had already reached the end of the hallway. I trotted to catch up.

We rounded the corner to the art room—

—and stopped dead.

"Oh, no." I closed my eyes.

Noah stared straight ahead. "Why is *she* here so early? And what is she *doing?*"

I shook my head. When it came to Sam Zawicki, I hardly ever knew what she was doing.

five

Sam had plastered herself against the bulletin board.

The Art Club bulletin board.

Her arms were splayed across the smooth red paper Mrs. Frazee had stapled over the cork, her army jacket flapping, her eyes burning a Zawicki Hole of Fury through the Kaleys—Kaley Timbrough and Kaley Crumm.

They stood side by side in their matching basketball warm-ups. Kaley C. shielded a cardboard cutout of the Fighting Aviator, school mascot, from Sam's glare. Kaley T. cradled an armful of photos against her chest. Mrs. Frazee's neat cutout letters had been ripped from the bulletin board and were scattered across the floor at their feet:

A, R, T, C, L, U, B, A, C, H, I, E, V, E, M, E, N, T, S.

And then my eyes lit on someone else.

I froze.

She was crouched among the letters, scrambling to retrieve them. Her shiny hair shimmered as she reached for a bent letter C. Her shiny pink nails glimmered as she shuffled the letters into a pile. Her shiny personality glistened through the early-morning gray of the Amelia M. Earhart Middle School hallway.

Emma.

For a minute I just stood there, bag of posters clamped so tight, my fingers had formed two solid dents in the Bristol board.

"It's not yours."

Sam's low snarl snapped me back to the known universe.

"You already own everything else in the stupid school," said Sam. "Keep your hands off this."

I blinked. What was she talking about?

The Kaleys shot each other a look that very clearly said, "Well, *yeah*. We're *supposed* to own the school."

Kaley C. gave Sam a sneery smile. "It is ours. Mr. Petrucelli gave it to us. Although we're going to have to do something about *that*." She pointed to a bent part of the metal frame that twanged cockeyed off the bulletin board. "Maybe we can cover it up with a banner."

I stared at her. That was *our* bulletin board. Bent and cockeyed maybe, but *ours*.

"It's not Mr. Petrucelli's to give." Sam narrowed her eyes. Her hair, crackling with static from rubbing up against the bulletin board, practically stood on end.

"It belongs to Art Club," said Sam.

"Oh, please. Art Club." Kaley T. rolled her eyes. "Like that's even a real thing."

"It is a real thing." Emma looked up from smoothing out a bent letter H. "It's a very important real thing to some people."

She flashed her half-dimple smile at me. I passed out temporarily.

I was quickly revived by a voice booming down the hall: "What is going on here?"

We turned to see Mr. Petrucelli striding toward us, serious principal face clenched in a serious principal frown, serious principal tie flapping with each step he took, seriously polished principal shoes clicking across the floor tiles.

He clicked to a stop in front of the bulletin board. "May I remind you that this is a place of learning?"

"No kidding." Sam took aim with her pointy chin. "We were just learning that the girls' basketball team is stealing the Art Club bulletin board."

"Art Club?" Mr. Petrucelli's serious principal forehead wrinkled into a frown. "We still have that?"

"Yes, we still have that," said Sam. "Ask *him*."

She jerked her chin toward me this time, and everyone turned to look.

At me, Tucker MacBean, undercover national contest winner.

The hum of the overhead lights buzzed in my ears. Their glare blurred my vision. The hall began to spin, and suddenly I was back in Bottenfield's: Sporty athletic people had stolen something, and now they were staring me down, daring me to get it back. While Emma Quinn watched.

I couldn't trust my mouth to say anything helpful. The best it had come up with last time was "I—uh—erg." So I did the only thing I could think of: produce evidence. I bent down to tug mangled cutouts from beneath Mr. Petrucelli's foot.

I held up three letters.

Mr. Petrucelli looked at them, confused.

"It's all this big misunderstanding," said Emma. "When we asked for a bulletin board, we didn't know you had to take it away from Art Club."

"Yes. Well." Mr. Petrucelli cleared his throat. "I didn't realize, either. But what's done is done."

Done? I stared at him. It couldn't be done. I had *posters*.

"You know what's done?" said Sam. "Basketball. They finished playing before winter break." She flung an arm toward the Kaleys. "They've already got the whole Athletic Department bulletin board by the front door. *And* a trophy case. Why do they need this board?"

Kaley T. rolled her eyes for about the hundredth time. "To commemorate our season. *Duh.*"

Sam skewered her with a glare. "You won two whole games. You want to commemorate *that?*"

"Yes. Well." Mr. Petrucelli cleared his throat again. "The girls worked hard, no matter what their record turned out to be, and we need to allocate bulletin board space to accommodate the greatest number of students."

Noah had been watching the whole time. Now he wrinkled his forehead in a confused frown. "So . . . they get the bulletin board because there are more of them?"

That was my friend, Noah Spooner: always ready with the math.

"Well, I wouldn't put it quite that way." Mr. Petrucelli straightened his tie. "But more students do participate in athletics."

Sam narrowed her eyes. "Fine," she said. "How many people do they need?"

Mr. Petrucelli was still fiddling with his tie. Now he stopped and pulled his chin back, like a rooster caught in midcluck. "What?"

Sam let out a breath. "You said Art Club doesn't have enough members. So how many do they need to get their bulletin board back?"

"I—no—it's not like that," said Mr. Petrucelli. "I don't have a figure—"

Sam turned to Emma. "How many girls on the basketball team?"

"Both seventh and eighth grade?" said Emma. "Nineteen."

Sam turned back to Mr. Petrucelli. "So if Art Club gets nineteen members, they get their bulletin board back."

Kaley T. rolled her eyes again. "Like *that's* going to happen."

Kaley C. let out a snort. "Nobody's even *heard* of Art Club."

I stared at her.

Because *yeah*, nobody had heard of Art Club. How could they? It's not like Art Club had uniforms and cheerleaders and a marching band and encouraging cutout posters plastered to our lockers and fans cheering us on. If we did, there'd already be as many Art Club members as basketball players. More, probably, since Art Club didn't have to run suicides up and down the bleachers. But all we'd ever had was a lousy bulletin board in the electives hallway, and now we weren't even going to have that.

While my brain was busy thinking that stuff,

my mouth was doing something else entirely. Here's what my mouth was doing:

"We'll have a pep assembly," it said.

Sam stared at me. She pierced me with a Zawicki Glare of What-the-Heck-Is-*Wrong*-with-You-Bean-boy?

Noah shot me a confused frown, clearly wondering if I knew what I was doing.

Kaley C. rolled her eyes again. "That's just stupid," she said.

"No, it's not," said my mouth, even though the rest of me was pretty sure it was. "An Art Club pep assembly so that everyone will finally know about us and see what we're doing and maybe get excited, at least a little bit, some of them anyway, to find out there's a club they might want to join, where they could maybe win a contest, a prestigious, *national* contest. And even if they don't, they could at least—"

"Look." Mr. Petrucelli folded his serious principal arms over his chest. "It's nice that you want to drum up business for your little club, but we can't interrupt the school day for a pep assembly. We're already going to miss class time gearing up for the school carnival. Students need to be in class learning."

"But"—Emma frowned—"we had pep assemblies every Friday during basketball."

"That was different," said Mr. Petrucelli. "The entire student body—"

"And football. And volleyball," said Emma. "And wrestling. Fair is fair, Mr. P."

She beamed her mind-jamming superpower over Mr. Petrucelli.

He looked at her, then at the Kaleys, who stood side by side, arms crossed over their basketball warm-ups, rage snorting out of their nostrils. Then at me, with my trash bag. He let out a breath. Pinched the little knob of stress that had bulged up between his eyebrows. "Fine," he said. "You can have your little pep assembly. Twenty minutes, Friday afternoon, just before school lets out."

"Great," I said out loud.

Crud, I said inside.

six

"A *pep* assembly?" I hopped on one foot as I dug my lunch card from my shoe. "What was I thinking?"

Noah and I inched along the line into the cafeteria. Around us, Earhart Middle School students talked and laughed. The squawk of voices and clank of silverware echoed off the painted cinder block walls.

"I'm not peppy. I don't know anything about cheers or jumping or"—I stopped, my voice choked off by a sudden alarming thought—"pom-poms. Oh, man. *Pom-poms?*" I stared at Noah, my eyes too horrified to blink. "I can't do pom-poms."

"Actually"—Noah pulled a lunch tray from the top of the stack—"pom-poms *are* standard pep assembly gear, but I don't think they're required."

Would this make *you* join Art Club?

I shook my head. I hoped he was right. I picked up a tray, clanked a fork and spoon onto it, and held it up so one of the lunch ladies could glob a mound of macaroni onto it.

The last thing Tucker MacBean, Real Live Person, needed was to stand in the middle of the gym, in front of bleachers packed with fellow students, and let his dweebery ooze out for everyone to see.

oozing
dweebery

dweeb
puddles

I held out my tray for carrot sticks and apple-sauce, then followed Noah toward our table.

In middle school, lunchroom seating patterns get established the first day, and they're pretty much locked into place for the whole year. Noah and I were locked into our table by the (fragrant) trash bins. Sam and her brother, Dillon, were locked into their table under the sputtering Exit sign.

Most days Sam and Dillon didn't say much to each other. Just sat there, hunkered over their lunch sacks, chewing their peanut butter sandwiches in silence.

But today, for some reason, Sam was talking. Boy, was she talking. She and Dillon were on the other side of the lunchroom, and I couldn't hear anything over the rumble, but whatever she was saying, she meant it. She'd planted her elbows in the center of the table and was leaned across it, her back rigid, her hair rigid too, her face so far up in Dillon's, they were practically eyelash to eyelash. She was a whole lot smaller than Dillon, of course—a sparrow going up against a water buffalo—but she was a fierce sparrow, her face pinched and serious. Dillon hunched his shoulders and coiled back, shielding himself from the cannon blast of her voice.

I almost felt sorry for him. I mean, he was Dillon Zawicki and everything, so you couldn't feel *too* sorry for him or he'd hit you.

But Sam in your face—not fun.

I was just glad she wasn't in *my* face this time. She probably would be later.

I wove my way through the tables.

Wesley Banks was sprawled in his usual chair next to T.J. and Luke, his legs stretched out in the narrow aisle between the tables so that anybody leaving the lunch line had to step over his jumbo basketball shoes to get to their table.

The Kaleys sat there, too, of course.

And Emma.

As I waited for Noah to climb over Wesley's shoes, Emma turned and beamed her shininess at me, full on.

"Hey, Tucker," she said. Her voice sounded shiny, too, like a shiny silver bell.

"I—uh—hey," I managed to choke out. Which, for me, was pretty conversational.

"Hey, *Tut*." Another voice cut through the shininess. Not silvery like a bell. Gravelly, like a meat grinder.

I turned. They were all looking at me. Wesley. Luke. T.J. Smiling their smirky smiles. The Kaleys too.

"Oh. Hey," I said back. I didn't mean it, of course. But I said it.

Wesley kept his gaze on me, steady, daring me to do . . . something, it seemed like. I didn't get *what*.

Till I started climbing over his feet.

He'd been sitting there the whole time, not moving a flick. And now, suddenly, as I started to climb over, as I balanced my tray in my hands—the milk, the silverware, the macaroni, carrots, and applesauce—as I lifted my foot to climb over, in that instant, the jumbo basketball shoes jerked—not a lot, just a little, enough to knock my leg right out from under me.

I stumbled. Tried to catch myself. My tray flailed wildly, carrots shooting one way, silverware another. Applesauce splashed from its neat square compartment onto my face and down my front. My milk carton teetered and for a second I teetered, too, with nothing to hold me up. Somebody grabbed me from behind, I think—I don't know who—grabbed my shirt, pulled me back. Otherwise I would've skidded across the Amelia M. Earhart Middle School lunchroom on my face.

I took a breath. Steadied my tray. And myself. Applesauce dripped from my chin. Snickers and giggles echoed around me.

I cut a quick look behind me. Tried to figure out who'd saved me from falling on my face. The Sundances were the closest, but they weren't even looking at me. Luke was doubled over laughing—because yeah, Wesley was *sooooo* funny—and T.J. was busy chugging his milk.

"Oops." Wesley laughed. "Looks like you spilled something. You need some help?" He held up a wadded napkin.

I gritted my teeth. I tipped my milk carton back up so it wouldn't fall off the tray.

"I'm fine," I said.

I didn't meet his eyes.

I didn't meet Emma's, either. If she was laughing, laughing along with Wesley, along with T.J. and Luke and the Kaleys, along with the rest of Earhart Middle, I couldn't bear to see it. And I couldn't bear seeing her give me a sympathetic poor-Tucker look either.

I headed through the cafeteria, eyes locked on the ceiling, staring at the hoodie somebody had tossed over one of the light fixtures, so I wouldn't accidentally look into somebody's face.

"Hey, Tut." Wesley's voice rang out behind me. "Next time watch where you're going."

seven

After school, I sidled down the hall toward Art Club.

Probably nobody had heard about me and my big mouth and what it had blabbered to Mr. Petrucelli that morning. Probably Mr. Petrucelli had forgotten all about it anyway. Or had at least come to his senses and decided I was the last person on the planet he should put in charge of a pep assembly.

Probably I had nothing to worry about.

I slipped through the art room door—

—smack into a wave of cheers.

Not a *huge* wave of cheers. For that we'd need a huge wave of people, and as I blinked off my surprise, I realized the Kaleys were kind of right. We'd lost five kids over winter break: two moved away, one kid's parents made him drop out after he flunked study hall, one switched to Audiovisual Club, and one was banned from afterschool activities for burping the Pledge of Allegiance during a citizenship assembly. Art Club had dribbled down to nine members total, ten if you counted the dust-caked papier mâché Fighting Aviator moldering away on the bookshelf behind Mrs. Frazee's desk. Sam would thump me into the next galaxy for saying so, but if we only had nine members, maybe we *weren't* a real club anymore.

Mrs. Frazee swooped across the crunchy concrete floor, her wild red hair bobbing.

"I'm so proud of you, Tucker." She looped an arm over my shoulder. Her bangly turquoise bracelets clanked against my cheek. "A pep assembly—*brilliant!*"

Spencer Osterholtz stepped forward from the tiny mob of club members, a new stocking cap pulled over his head.

**Case File:
The Spencinator**

Status: I'm not sure they've invented a category Spencer fits into. He's clearly not a villain. At least, not intentionally. He'd like to be a hero. But I don't see that happening. He'd probably like to be a sidekick, too, if anyone would have him. For now I guess his status remains UNDETERMINED.

Base: Art Club.

Superpower: Relentless, single-minded determination. Often annoying to people around him, but, I have to admit, effective.

Superweapon: Sharp, flinging elbows; long, gangly feet on long, gangly legs; and complete and total klutziness. The main two problems with these weapons are (1) they don't have a lot of accuracy or any sort of control switch, and (2) they're more of a danger to Spencer than to anyone else.

Real Name: Spencer Osterholtz

Spencer pumped his fist in the air. "Go!"

Art Club let out a whoop and began hoisting themselves on top of one another.

And falling off.

And hoisting again.

I finally figured it out. They were trying to build a human pyramid. It looked more like sumo wrestling for the meek and undersized. Here's a clue about Art Club: we're not famous for our upper-body strength. The bottom layer of the pyramid gave a valiant effort, but their elbows just weren't up to the challenge. They quivered and wobbled, and when they ultimately gave out, the top layers crashed down on them.

Spencer wriggled out from under the pile. "So what do you think?" He peered up at me from the concrete. "Extreme, right?

"Oh—yeah," I said. "It was—I don't even—wow."

"Thanks." Spencer climbed to his feet. He hitched up his jeans and dusted chunks of dried clay and broken pencil lead from his knees.

He retrieved his stocking cap.

It was red and white and puffy, with earflaps and a perky yarn ball on the top. His great-aunt Bernice had clearly been busy again.

"We've been thinking up ideas all day," said Spencer. "Passing notes back and forth, talking between classes, with one pretty intense discussion at lunch. The pyramid was my idea." His bony chest puffed with pride. "We need to practice a little more, of course. Polish it up. Give it that extra puh-zing."

The Bernice Osterholtz
KNITWEAR COLLECTION

stocking cap

scarf

mittens

socks

cell phone case

He stopped. He gave me a concerned look. Probably because I was standing there with my mouth open.

"Or not," he said quickly. "We don't have to use it if you don't want to. I know you have your own ideas. You wouldn't have volunteered us for the pep assembly if you didn't, right?" He looked at me. "So, what's the plan?"

Plan? I stared at him. My plan was to tack posters on a bulletin board and maybe, possibly, fingers crossed, make art less invisible at Earhart Middle School.

Not get us all flushed down the toilet of middle school humiliation.

Art Club had gathered behind Spencer, watching me.

I swallowed. "Gosh, I don't want to, you know, take over the whole thing. I mean, since you guys had all this time to think up ideas, you probably came up with something even better than some crazy pep assembly, right? A beefed-up morning announcement maybe, or—hey!—a newsletter!"

Spencer frowned. "You don't want to do the pep assembly?" He shot a puzzled look at the rest of Art Club. "But we've been practicing."

Art Club nodded. Their admiration took a confused turn.

I closed my eyes. "I didn't say I don't *want* to. I just meant we should give it some thought—"

That was all it took. Spencer pumped his fist in the air once more, and suddenly everyone was cheering again. By the time Art Club was over, I'd been elected to stand on the top of the human pyramid, holding the papier mâché Fighting Aviator to demonstrate school spirit.

"*And*"—Spencer grabbed my arm as I was trying

to sidle out of the art room—"I've got a little extra puh-zing up *my* sleeve, too. I need to work out the details, but I promise, it'll be something you *never* expected."

eight

I darted from Earhart Middle—into a wall of winter. It wasn't even suppertime yet, but the weary January sun had already given up and was sliding down behind the rooftop of the school. I pulled up the hood of my coat and took off toward Quincy Street, clouds of white breath trotting along beside me.

And all of Art Club pressing down on my head.

Because yeah, the most pathetic pep assembly in recorded history was clearly the path to middle-school dominance.

I scooted down Quincy.

Through the park.

Across the tennis court.

Thought about hurdling the net.

Decided to go around. My mom didn't need the hospital bill.

I cut through the alley and popped out onto Polk Street. Our house stood on the corner, two stories of ancient brick and fussy white trim peering through the brittle, winter-bare branches of Polk Street's towering oaks.

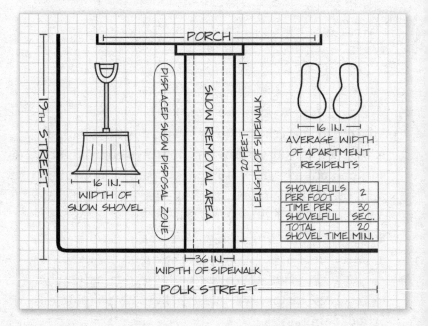

Joe and Samir had shoveled a path up our front walk using some mathematical calculation they'd invented that would (as Samir explained) "give our walkway the greatest amount of tread area while expending the least amount of human labor." Which I think was their scientific way of saying, "We're not shoveling any more than we have to."

Our house, like most of the old houses by the university, was split into apartments. Joe and Samir, two astronomy students, lived on the first floor. Rosalie, our resident music student and used-to-be go-to babysitter (before Sam Zawicki) (not that I needed a babysitter anymore) (but Beech still did), managed to stay cheery and musical in the festering sinkhole known as the basement apartment, despite the seepy windows and relentless chug and rattle of the boiler.

Mom, Beech, and I lived in the MacBean Family Apartment on the second floor, tucked snug under the eaves.

I stomped up the walk between Joe and Samir's piles of snow, across the porch, and into our first-floor entryway. I stood there for a few seconds to let the warmth seep into my frozen body, then hiked my backpack over my shoulder and thumped up the stairs.

I found them in the kitchen, Beecher sitting in his spot at the table, Sam at the sink, slicing an apple onto a plate. Beech didn't have his usual pillowcase tucked into his shirt as a cape. He hadn't worn his pillowcase cape since that day at Bottenfield's.

Sam slid the plate in front of him. He stared at it—at the apple pieces, arranged to make a nose, a mouth, and a pair of eyes, with little slivers for eyebrows and two raisins for the eyeballs—and let out a little squeal, like a happy chipmunk.

"Tool!" He gave Sam a look of pure adoration. "You rot," he said. "I tell Mrs. Hottins you rot."

Mrs. Hottins. His special ed teacher. He told Mrs. Hottins everything.

Just like he told Sam everything when she baby-sat him after school.

Just like he hardly told me anything these days.

His glasses had slid halfway down his nose. Sam pushed them up.

"*You* rock, kid," she told him.

Then she turned on me. Fired such a burning glare at me, I had to rub my cheeks to make sure they hadn't burst into flames.

"Of all the things you could've come up with," she said, "a pep assembly has to be the lamest."

"No kidding," I said.

"So." Sam crossed her arms over her army jacket. "How are you going to make it work?"

"Work?" I shook my head. "What are you talking about? You've seen Art Club. How could it possibly work?"

She let out an irritated breath. "I didn't say it *would*. It *might*. But only if you don't act like a complete doorknob."

She tipped her head toward Beecher, her ever-faithful lieutenant, who swallowed his apple chunk, wiped his hands on his jeans, and fished out a yellow sticky note from his pocket.

He slapped it on the table and gave a satisfied nod. "Note," he said.

I gave it a suspicious look. Whenever the two of them started coming up with ideas, it never turned out well for me.

I peeled the crumpled paper from the table.

I read through the list. "So . . . no cheers, no pom-poms—"

Sam stabbed me with a glare. "You bring a pom-pom anywhere near this assembly, I'll rip your bulletin board down myself."

"Hey." I held up my hands. "I'm way ahead of you. What's this?" I pointed to the last item on the list.

"Oh. Yeah," she said. "You know how before games they hold up a giant paper banner and the team runs out and crashes through it and everybody cheers? Whoopee. The biggest guys in our school can beat up paper." She narrowed her eyes. "You better not do anything that sorry."

Especially since there was no guarantee Art Club *could* beat up paper.

"But"—I looked back at the list—"if we take out all this stuff, there's nothing left. Except my posters, which are excellent, I admit, but they won't make much of a bang at a pep assembly."

"You're such a Beanboy sometimes." Sam forced out a breath. "You art people are supposed to be creative, right?"

"Yeah."

"So create. You think anybody's going to pay attention if you do all that cheer stuff anyway? They've already seen it a hundred times, done by people way more coordinated than Art Club. You want them to pay attention, you can't do the same things cheerleaders do only pathetically worse. You have to do things different."

"But see?" I said. "That's the point. Art Club *does* do things different. *Way* different." I pasted the sticky note back on the table. "We're not pep assembly material. We're more like . . . *anti*–pep assembly material.

If you want to help, make a list of how to convince *them* how stupid this whole assembly thing is. They're all hyped up about a human pyramid. I have to figure out how to talk them out of it."

Sam stood there looking at me, not even glaring, just standing there with her mouth open and nothing coming out.

Something I never thought I'd see in my lifetime.

"So that's it?" she said finally. "You're not doing the assembly? You're just going to wimp out? On your own club?"

Beecher chewed his apple and watched me.

"What? No," I said. "I'm not wimping out. I'm facing facts."

"That's what wimps say."

I blinked. What was wrong with her? Nobody hated school spirit more than Sam Zawicki. She *really* hated pep assemblies, and now here she was, yelling at me about doing one. It was like the planet had hit some turbulence and now we were all spinning in the wrong direction.

She shook her head. "I figured this would happen."

She hoisted her satchel onto the counter and unfastened the flap.

"I did some stuff of my own," she said.

She pulled out a stack of tall, thin library books

and set them on her satchel. She opened the top book, riffled through till she found the page she wanted, then shoved it at me.

I balanced the book in my hands and studied the shiny page of black-and-white photos. It was a yearbook. I turned it over to see the cover. Amelia M. Earhart Middle School. An old one from a long time ago, like fifteen years, before I was born, even.

Sam planted her fists on her hips. "So? What do you see?"

I scrutinized the page. "The top one is a picture of Stamp Collecting Enthusiasts. Below that is Marble Club, posing with their favorite marbles, it looks like." I glanced at the opposite page. "Science Fiction Book Club. And—*wow*—Square Dance Club? Who wears clothes like that on purpose?"

"Yeah. Embarrassing. Keep going."

I turned the page.

And stopped dead.

"Comic Book Collectors?"

I stared at the photo at the top of the page. Mostly guys, with a couple of girls, all clustered around a bulletin board, holding comic books. A tall guy clutching a Wonder Woman comic book looked kind of familiar, but I couldn't figure out why.

"Earhart Middle had a Comic Book Collectors Club?" I said. "Why didn't anyone tell me? I would completely be in a club like that."

"How many members?"

"What? I don't know." I counted the kids in the photo. "Fifteen. Why?"

She didn't say anything. Just slid the next year-book off the stack and handed it to me, opened to a page of pictures.

"Hey." I tapped my finger on a photo. "Here they are again."

"That's the next year. How many members?"

I counted. "Eleven."

Sam slid another yearbook onto my stack, open to Comic Book Collectors. "This is the year after that."

"Nine," I said.

She handed me the final yearbook. I paged through it. Paged through again. Then again, scrambling the pages this time.

↑ Square Dance Club here

* ← Notice anything missing here?

↓ Science Fiction Book Club here

"Where did they go?" I said, sort of frantically. "What happened to the Comic Book Collectors?"

Sam held up her hands. "Who knows? They had nine members that last time. Then the next year—gone."

"Gone? Are you sure?" I shuffled through the pages one more time. "Did they ever show up again?"

"Have you noticed a Comic Book Club at school?"

I shook my head.

"They're gone."

"Oh, *man*." A sudden thought hit me. I slumped back against the refrigerator, open yearbook against my chest. "*Art Club* only has nine members."

"No kidding. Notice anything else?"

She pulled the next-to-last yearbook from the stack and jabbed a finger at the Comic Book Collectors picture, the one with only nine members. But she didn't jab at the kids. She jabbed at the background.

A background that looked familiar.

"Oh, man. Oh, no." I stared at it.

The Comic Book Collectors stood on both sides of the bulletin board, holding comic books: H2O, Batman, Captain America, even Archie. A bent part of the metal bulletin board frame twanged cockeyed off to the side.

"That's *our* bulletin board," I said. "Art Club's." I peered at the picture. "It used to belong to *them?* To Comic Book Collectors?"

Sam nodded.

I closed my eyes. "Art Club is doomed."

Sam closed the yearbooks and slid them back into her satchel. "And you're just going to wimp out on them."

Beech nodded. "Wimp out."

"What? No. I'm not."

"So you're doing the pep assembly," said Sam.

"Well, yeah. I mean, I guess I have to." I narrowed my eyes. "And anyway, why are *you* so worried about it?"

"What?" Sam pulled her chin back. Gave me a weird look. "I'm not worried. It's not even my stupid club." She heaved her satchel over her shoulder. "But I stuck my neck out this morning. I made Mr. Petrucelli say he'd give the bulletin board back if you dug up more people. I'm going to look stupid if you don't step up. And I will *not* look stupid. Got it?"

She shot me one more burning glare and snapped her green winter parka from the hook by the door.

"Now I have to take care of whatever stupid thing Dillon's been up to," she muttered as she banged out of the kitchen and down the stairs.

nine

Different. Art Club was different.

As the echo of Sam's boots faded away and the front door downstairs slammed shut behind her, I thought about this.

We *couldn't* do the same things cheerleaders did. We had to do different things.

I wiped apple slime off Beech's hands. And mouth. And eyebrows. Then I bundled him up in his winter coat and snow boots and dragged him through the cold and slush, back through the park toward Quincy Street.

The main difference between Art Club and cheerleaders: Art Club didn't work in front of a crowd. We didn't jump up and down. We didn't do art in your face. Well, maybe Spencer. But mostly, we worked in private. That's what we were good at. If this pep assembly—no, this *anti*–pep assembly—had even the slimmest chance of working, we had to do things we were good at.

We finally reached Caveman Comics. Beecher stopped dead in surprise.

"Superhero." His awestruck whisper floated out on a puff of white breath. *"Tool."*

The stairway at Caveman Comics was the only set of steps in the whole world of Beecher MacBean that he would willingly walk down without screaming. He wrapped one mittened hand around the railing, the other around my wrist—about cut off my circulation—and trooped down the steps, dragging me along with him.

We reached the bottom and pushed through the door. The bell jangled against the glass.

Caveman didn't look up, even though we barreled in on a blast of chill wind that ruffled the covers of his comic books. He was planted on the stool behind the back counter, hunched over a graphic novel. He never moved from that spot. Never came out from behind the counter. I was pretty sure he had legs, but I'd never seen them.

Beech shot like a bullet toward a Batman display. I scuffed across the thin, wrinkled carpet toward the rack beside the cash register. One of Caveman's homemade signs was thumb-tacked above it:

NEW ARRIVALS

I scanned the rack. Batman. Superman. Avengers. Spidey. No H2O. No big introduction of H2O's awesome new sidekick, Beanboy. I ran my finger down the printout Caveman had tacked up beside the rack:

COMING SOON

Still no H2O. I glanced behind the counter. Except for a slight flutter of his shaggy black hair when he breathed, Caveman hadn't moved. You wouldn't know it by talking to him, since his main form of communication was a reluctant grunt, but if you needed to know anything about any comic book anywhere, Caveman was your guy.

You just had to work up enough courage to ask him.

I casually leaned against the counter. "So. Hey," I said.

He didn't look up.

"I was just wondering if you had any idea when the next H2O comic book would be here. *Episode Ten* in the H2O Submerged series, with his new sidekick, Beanboy. That one."

He still didn't look up. He just jerked his sausage of a finger toward the COMING SOON printout.

"Yeah." I nodded. "But it's not on the list."

Caveman licked his finger and turned a page in his novel.

Which probably meant the conversation was over.

"See, the thing is," I said, "I really need to know."

He didn't move.

"I've got this, well, situation. At school. See, I'm in Art Club, and we really need to impress people. At an assembly. The comic book contest would be *really* impressive, except nobody knows about it, and probably they wouldn't believe me even if I told them. Unless I had the actual comic book in my hands. But I don't know when it'll be out. The comic book company hasn't told me, and I don't know who to ask. And now that we lost our bulletin board—"

Caveman's head popped up. He peered at me from under his one long dark ledge of an eyebrow (which partially explains his name). I jumped back, startled. He'd never actually looked me in the eye before.

"You lost your bulletin board?" he said.

I blinked. That was the longest sentence I'd ever heard him utter. For a few seconds I didn't know what to do.

"Um, yeah," I said finally. "I know it probably doesn't sound like a big deal, and it's not even that great a bulletin board, with the frame all bent like it is—"

"Bent?"

I nodded. "But it turned into this whole big thing—"

"It always does."

"Yeah." I frowned. "But the thing is, if I could get my hands on that comic book, I mean, really soon, like, what do they call it, an advance copy or something—"

"I'll see what I can do."

I stopped. He'd see what he could do?

I guess the conversation was truly over then, because he buried his head in his novel again, and his shaggy hair didn't even flutter.

"So, okay," I said. "Thanks. Any idea when that might be?"

Nothing.

"I mean, I was just kind of wondering. So I could plan my schedule around it."

Still nothing.

Beech had trotted over while I was lounged against the counter, and now he held up a set of shiny plastic Batarangs. He didn't say anything. Just held them up.

The way he was looking at them, with utter love—not as much love as he had for the batting helmet, of course—and with his eyes all big with hope, I couldn't even bring myself to try to talk him out of it. I just dug my emergency relief fund from my shoe and slapped the money on the counter.

Caveman deposited it, slid the Batarangs into a plastic bag, and handed me the receipt, all without taking his eyes off his graphic novel. I handed Beech the bag and we headed out of the shop.

As we started up the steps, I turned and glanced back through the dusty glass door. Caveman was holding his place in his graphic novel with his finger. But he'd lifted his head again and was staring at his COMING SOON list and chewing his lip in thought.

Giving Beecher MacBean pointy superhero throwing weapons.

Possibly not my best idea.

ten

I swallowed the hard lump in my throat. "So that's the plan," I said.

I stood before Art Club, my page of ideas clamped to a clipboard I'd rustled up from my mom's desk to give it a more official look. And also to keep my hands steady. I'd laid everything out for them, tapping each item on the list for emphasis: the *anti*–pep assembly, doing the opposite, creating most of it here in the art room ahead of time, being there at the pep assembly to direct the action and look totally cool, but letting our work stand for itself.

Plus no pom-poms.

Art Club stared back at me. Dead silent. Even the papier mâché Fighting Aviator looked stunned.

Spencer sat perched on the edge of his tall art stool, not moving, a stack of papers clutched between his hands.

Gretchen Klamm, who spent her Art Club time weaving artistic belts, sank back in her seat. I knew why—she had collapsed from sheer disappointment.

Then she threw her fist in the air. "Yes! Thank you!" She turned to the rest of Art Club. "I'm sorry. I know you guys wanted to lead the school in art cheers and everything, but the more I thought about it, the more lightheaded I got. If I have to stand out there and do those dance kicks we were trying to make up, I'm serious, I would pass out."

"No kidding," said Martin Higby. "Just thinking about it makes me dizzy."

Art Club all started talking at once.

"I thought I was going to throw up."

"I broke out in *hives*."

"Last time we tried the human pyramid, I think I sprained my armpit."

Now I was the one who was stunned. Art Club was *happy* about the anti–pep assembly. Mrs. Frazee got so excited, she about knocked herself unconscious with her jangly earrings.

"Tucker. You realize what you're suggesting, don't you?" She clapped a hand to her chest. Her bracelets clanked with joy. "Performance art!"

She swooped to the shelves behind her desk, rummaged through, and, in triumph, pulled a large book from one of the piles. She blew dust from the cover and settled it on the center worktable, then opened it to a page of shiny photos showing people doing things that were, well, odd but also pretty interesting. Bald guys with their heads painted blue on a stage with some . . . plumbing, it looked like, only it was kind of like sculpture, too. And another bunch of people wearing brightly colored tights, squeezed into different small spaces, like doorways and windows and stuff, till they almost looked like a painting. A living painting.

"Performance art." Mrs. Frazee fairly breathed the words. "Combining visual art, the kind we do right here in Art Club—painting, drawing, sculpture— with dramatic performance. You can use all kinds of different media—music, film, TV screens, computers—nearly anything you can think of to convey your idea to the world."

As she stood beside the worktable, explaining, Mrs. Frazee practically turned into performance art herself. Her wild red hair danced like a moving sculpture. Her handmade jewelry jingled, and her hand-dyed scarf swished in musical accompaniment. Her voice rose dramatically till it filled the art room.

"You can do performance art anywhere. On stage,

in public places, or"—she paused for dramatic effect—"in a middle school gymnasium."

Mrs. Frazee gushed on about performance art. I was still stuck on the first thing she'd said: *Convey your idea.* That's exactly what we were trying to do: Convey the idea that Art Club was important. That we still existed. That we deserved a bulletin board just as much as the basketball team.

Maybe we *were* doing performance art.

Accidentally.

Mrs. Frazee closed the book with a thud. The rest of Art Club scrambled to get started on our anti–pep assembly.

I stood there, in the middle of the art room, thinking maybe my mouth had known what it was doing when it blabbered to Mr. Petrucelli about a pep assembly . . .

. . . and gazed right into the eyes of Spencer Osterholtz.

He still sat on his art stool, clenching his papers. His hand-knitted stocking cap drooped over his ears. He attempted a smile, but it was pretty weak.

"I was right," he said. "You *did* have a plan. I knew you did, because you wouldn't volunteer us for a pep assembly if you didn't, right? So you were just waiting to show it to us till you'd spiffed it up, given it that extra puh-zing. And wow, did you give it puh-zing. I couldn't even imagine that much puh-zing. An *anti*–pep assembly that turns out to be performance art *and* turns into a whole new lesson plan for Mrs. Frazee. Wow."

He took a breath. He tried to act all positive and cheery. But his shoulders had slumped. His stocking cap was deflated.

"All I came up with was that dumb human pyramid," he said.

"Hey." I gave him an encouraging fist bump to the arm. "It wasn't that dumb."

He stared at a blob of tempera paint on the concrete floor. "But it doesn't really fit in anymore. These don't fit now, either." He started to crumple the papers in his hand.

ATTENTION, ART CLUB

To kick this thing up a notch, give it some real PUH-ZING, we need the following:

1. A new twist on the traditional pom-pom: special artistic KNITTED pom-poms (just say the word, and my great-aunt will be on it).

2. A catchy Art Club theme song we could sing while doing our kick line—so catchy it gets stuck in everyone's head so the whole school will walk around for days afterward humming the tune and thinking about Art Club.

3. A grand finale for our human pyramid: At the end, we'll toss the top layer (which, in case anyone has forgotten, consists of Tucker) into the air (the higher the better for maximum visual impact), then catch him. This will give new meaning to the Amelia M. Earhart Middle School Fighting Aviators.

:)

"No, wait," said my mouth (because, seriously, you can never trust it to just shut up). "Let me see."

He opened his hand. I took the papers and smoothed out the crumples.

Spencer had typed it neatly on his computer and printed enough copies for everyone in Art Club.

"Some of this might still fit in," I said.

Spencer looked up, hopeful. "Like the knitted pom-poms?"

"Well, no. But this"—I tapped on #2—"a theme song. This could work. We probably wouldn't want to sing it because we'll be pretty busy doing other stuff."

Plus, I'd heard Art Club sing, and it didn't fit in with anything in the known universe.

"But we'll need a theme song playing behind us," I said, "backing us up."

Spencer's shoulders de-slumped. His stocking cap puffed up.

"That *would* fit in," he said.

"It would more than fit in," I said. "It would give us puh-zing."

eleven

We got help from Audiovisual Club, borrowed spot-lights from Drama Club, and talked Coach Wilder (football coach and health sciences teacher) into let-ting us use his sound system.

He was nervous about turning middle-schoolers loose with expensive electronic equipment, so when we borrowed the system, we sort of borrowed Coach Wilder along with it.

At first he just hovered around us as we worked, making sure no one accidentally stuck a tongue in a light socket or something.

Once he got a whiff of what we were trying to do, he started tossing out suggestions—suggestions that were surprisingly good for a guy whose brain spent so much time cooped up in a mildew-infested locker room.

"Squirrel-cage fans," he growled. He was standing beside the sound system, beefy arms folded across his chest like giant sausages squeezed into a gray sweatshirt. "What you need are squirrel-cage fans. And footlights."

We frowned, nodded, and gave one another confused looks. What the heck were squirrel-cage fans?

"Don't worry about it." Coach Wilder pulled a stubby pencil from behind his ear and a small, grubby notebook from the pocket of his workout pants. "I got connections."

He worked his jaw for a minute, licked the pencil lead, scribbled something in the notebook, and gave a solid, football-coach nod. He tucked his notebook back in his pocket.

The next day, when we got to Art Club, there they were: four huge metal fans that looked like enormous hamster wheels and a row of small, portable lights, lined up along the floor.

Coach Wilder was right. They were *exactly* what we needed.

I dragged Noah into the action. He wasn't a member of Art Club, but we needed a theme song, and Noah knew everything about music.

(Everything about everything, really. If Art Club

decided to recite medieval poetry or launch a satellite into space, Noah Spooner would be our man.)

Once Noah and Coach Wilder put their heads together, they were like the Dr. Frankensteins of the anti–pep assembly soundtrack. Coach had a whole collection of stadium jams. They riffled through to pick the best tunes. They collected drumbeats. They recorded sound effects. They hooked Noah's laptop into Coach Wilder's system and mixed and taped and edited and calibrated and pieced the parts together into a monster of thundering sound. Noah, like a true mad scientist, documented every step in his logbook.

Finally, when the monster was ready, they flipped a switch and let it roar.

Art Club shot one another raised-eyebrow looks, mouths open.

Because it was perfect. Their monster soundtrack instantly took our anti–pep assembly to a whole new level.

Spencer shot me a thumbs-up. "Puh-zing," he mouthed.

I nodded.

By the time Friday rolled around, Art Club was ready.

twelve

I inched the door open and pressed one eye against the crack. Art Club squeezed in behind me in our dank, dark hole (a.k.a. the boys' locker room), trying to steal a glimpse of the packed gym beyond.

Talking, laughing clumps of Earhart middle-schoolers had begun filing in. Their sneakers squeaked against the gym floor and thudded up the steps as they filled the bleachers. The rumble of voices swelled to fill every space in the gym, and the locker room door fairly quivered with the noise.

I sucked in a breath of the cool gym air that wafted through the crack and tried to push my pounding heart back into my chest. It had already siphoned all the blood from my brain, so now my head sort of floated above my body, numb and useless.

The video screens we'd built—the enormous main screen in the center, with two smaller screens on each side—were suspended securely from the gym ceiling, thanks to a very tall ladder, Coach Wilder, and some cables he'd rustled up from somewhere. He'd cranked the basketball goals up to the ceiling to make room. (And pulled down three pairs of dangling gym socks and a backpack while he was at it. It was getting weird. Almost every day something was hanging from the ceiling somewhere.) Once the gym lights went down and our video was beamed out, nobody would notice our amazing screens were just white paper enforced with stapled cardboard frames.

We'd placed the Drama Club spotlights at strategic points in the gym. Audiovisual Club had taken up their post behind the projectors at the top of the bleachers. Mrs. Frazee had appropriated my clipboard and now stood off to the side, where she could follow the action and get the whole thing back on track if it jumped the rails. Noah and Coach Wilder were stationed behind the sound system at the scorer's table on the opposite side of the gym, ready to put the whole thing in motion.

As I stood there, waiting, I heard the first glimmer of music. It started low, so low I doubt the rumbling herd in the gym even heard it at first. It grew louder—gradually—till by the time the crowd realized what they were hearing, it had become part of the very air around them.

This was no cheery marching band tune. This was darker, with a thundering beat. More tortured super-hero than perky pep squad.

The music swelled, louder and more insistent, till it blanketed the gym in a layer of sound. Voices dwindled as the crowd stopped talking and began listening. Exactly as Noah had predicted. The drums beat louder. Faster. Then—

BAM!

—the music stopped.

The gym went black.

Silence echoed through the dark.

As the crowd gasped and a few nervous giggles pierced the cavernous darkness, Art Club slipped silently from the locker room and stole along the edge of the gym. I led the way, head still numb, heart still pounding, my feet laced snug inside black combat boots.

I am normally not a combat boot sort of person. A basic pair of all-purpose sneakers takes me anywhere I need to go. But yesterday, after I'd gotten home from Art Club, after Sam had thumped out of our apartment and down the stairs, I'd headed to my room to dump my backpack—

—and found this pair of boots standing at attention in the hall outside my door, spit-polished and gleaming.

Beecher had motioned his head toward the boots. "Sam." That's all he'd said.

Now as I paced through the blackness of the gym, the heft of the combat boots swinging with each step I took, carrying my feet along almost without effort, I understood why Sam wore them. They made me feel taller somehow. Steadier. More powerful.

I took my place behind the row of footlights spaced along the edge of the gym floor. Art Club lined up beside me, and the music grew softer till it was merely a background for the sound effects: the roar and pop of a fire.

The footlights surged on, glowing orange and yellow. Coach Wilder's squirrel fans whirred. We'd cut flames from tissue paper and taped them to the front of the lights, and now the fans whipped them straight into the air. The tissue flames danced before the glowing lights, and suddenly the whole side of the gym looked like it was ablaze.

The crowd gasped. Art Club strode forward, calmly, through the flames. We didn't run. We didn't try to get through quickly. No. We stalked through fire itself, almost in slow motion, as flames licked our boots, our fingertips, our black cargo pants.

And as we strode through the flames, Audiovisual

Club projected the video of it directly onto our giant screen, with close-ups on the smaller screens at the sides, so that no matter where you looked, Art Club was rising from the flames.

The music grew louder and we strode to our assigned positions. I took my place behind one of the spotlights.

A giant image of Gretchen Klamm's best woven belt beamed onto the center screen, with video of her weaving it on the smaller screens, with dramatic lighting, quick cuts between shots, and music thundering.

I swung my light around. Beamed it directly onto Gretchen, standing beside a display of her art, so she was in the spotlight at the same moment she was on the screens, a lone Art Club member lit in stark contrast to the surrounding darkness.

New artwork played on the screens: Martin Higby's souped-up drawings of his dream racing machines. I dimmed my light as one of the other spotlights shone on short, round Martin, the last kid in the world you'd picture inside a race car.

The cars dimmed and new artwork filled the screens. Another spotlight shone on the artist.

Our black silhouettes were visible so the crowd could see we were in charge, moving the lights, directing the action. But the main action happened on the screens, with the photos and videos we'd put together—artwork, field trips, dazzling shots of paintings we'd seen at the Wheaton University Art Museum.

I stood behind my light, operating it smoothly, the way we'd practiced.

Still, I managed to sneak a peek at the bleachers.

And you know what?

Earhart Middle was watching. Sitting forward, eyes locked onto the screens, watching as images flashed and faded. I looked for Emma. Looked to see if she was sitting forward, eyes locked on to the screens too.

I couldn't find her but I saw another kid, a kid so entranced, so captivated, he had his hands clasped tight together and was holding them to his chin, so tight, so stiff, he was practically shaking.

I blinked. I knew that shake.

It was Beecher.

That shaking kid was Beecher.

And he was sitting beside . . . my mother. She saw me looking at her and gave me a wave and a giant really-proud-mom thumbs-up.

The music thundered. The video changed.

That was my cue.

I swiveled my spotlight and shone it directly on Spencer, whose coil pots were playing on the screens.

We were almost at the halfway point, almost to the part about my comic book, the part where Art Club would beam their spotlights on me, ending with an animation that Audiovisual Club had helped put together, of Beanboy (the real Beanboy, not me) soaring through the skies above Amelia M. Earhart Middle School. It was really nice of them to do that. Extreme, as Noah would say. It was completely extreme.

And standing there in my combat boots, holding my spotlight steady, I started to relax a little. I don't know what I'd been so worried about. I'd spent all that time convinced that this pep assembly thing would hurl Art Club down the middle school toilet of humiliation, and instead it might be the answer to everything.

It could get kids to sign up for Art Club.

We could become visible in our own school. We could get our bulletin board back. And Emma—I flicked another covert glance toward the bleachers—maybe next time Emma said, "Hey, Tucker," maybe I'd actually—

Bam!

The music screeched to a stop.

The video screens went dark and our spotlights faded to black.

Then the gym lights snapped on, full power.

As the entire school blinked under the glare of the suddenly bright gym, the cheerleading squad bounced onto the floor, chanting and shaking their pom-poms.

thirteen

Mr. Petrucelli bounded onto the floor, swiping the microphone from Coach Wilder's sound system as he jogged past.

"Thank you." He held up a hand. "Thank you."

His microphone squealed. The cheerleaders stopped cheering. They still bounced and shook their pom-poms (they were cheerleaders; they couldn't help themselves), just not as noisily.

I stood there gripping my spotlight, stupidly flipping the switch back and forth, as if our anti–pep assembly would magically start back up again if I could just get the dang light to come back on.

I guess we all thought that. Noah tapped furiously on the keys of his laptop. Audiovisual Club jiggled their projectors. Coach Wilder squeezed out from behind the sound system, Mrs. Frazee threw down her clipboard, and the two of them stalked across the gym floor, aimed like lasers straight at Mr. Petrucelli.

Mr. Petrucelli didn't seem to notice. "Very nice. Let's give them all a nice round of applause." He flashed his wide principal smile and waved an arm in the general direction of Art Club, who mostly stood paralyzed, mouths open in shock. Earhart Middle, still squinting under the bright gym lights, clapped politely.

Mr. Petrucelli got down to business. "We don't want to waste precious learning time on just one club, so this afternoon we're combining the Art Club assembly with an end-of-season pep rally for our basketball teams. Give it up for the Earhart Middle School Fighting Aviators."

Before we knew what was happening, the pep band marched into the gym, blaring the school fight song. About mowed down Coach Wilder and Mrs. Frazee, who had to scramble for their lives. The cheerleaders danced, revved up now to maximum cheering fervor.

The side doors banged open and a thundering pack of basketball players bounded onto the floor, Wesley Banks leading the boys from one side, the Kaleys leading the girls from the other. As I watched in horror, I realized both lines were barreling straight toward the screens.

And they didn't stop.

Didn't slow down.

They charged right toward the screens, *our* screens, the screens we'd spent an entire week constructing—

—and crashed through.

I stared at the shreds, at the wobbling frames.

The toughest kids in our school had just beat up paper.

Our paper.

Earhart Middle erupted in cheers.

I stood there in my combat boots, the noise and glaring gym lights spinning around me, and clutched my spotlight.

fourteen

Mr. Petrucelli's voice boomed through the microphone. "These teams worked hard, both the boys and the girls, and even though their seasons may not have turned out the way they planned, they deserve our support for a job well done."

Earhart Middle cheered.

I glanced up at the bleachers.

At my mom, who was standing up, standing straight up in the sea of middle-schoolers, beaming all her fury at Mr. Petrucelli's head.

Part of me wanted her to come charging across the gym, rip the microphone from Mr. Petrucelli's hand, get the anti–pep assembly going again, and make everything go the way it was supposed to go.

Maybe even wrap her arms around me and give me a really hard hug.

That part of me was still three years old.

The other part, the part that was thirteen, wished my mother didn't have to see what a pathetic loser I was and feel sorry for me.

Beecher stood at her side. All he looked was confused.

I rolled my spotlight toward the edge of the gym, picking up the cord as I went so I could unplug it once I got to the electric socket in the corner.

Behind me, the microphone squealed again.

"As you all know"—Mr. Petrucelli's voice blared— "the school carnival is coming up in a few short weeks."

Earhart Middle cheered. Again.

"That's right. That's right." Mr. Petrucelli waited while the gym quieted down. "It's one of the biggest events of the year, and I know our teams and clubs will be spending these next weeks getting their booths and games ready."

Art Club didn't have much to get ready. We were doing face painting. We always did face painting. We were Art Club. People expected face painting.

"And of course I know you'll all be flexing your throwing arms for the one carnival event everyone looks forward to—Amelia M. Earhart Middle School's annual Last Player Standing!"

The gym exploded in cheers. Earhart Middle pounded their feet against the bleachers. Cheerleaders shook their pom-poms and kicked really high. One of the tuba players blasted out a rumbly toot.

Earhart Middle loved the dodgeball tournament.

I liked it, too. From the sidelines. Where I could cheer others on. Where I was not the target of a rubber ball hurled eight hundred miles per hour straight at my gut.

"This year, we have something extra to get you fired up," said Mr. Petrucelli. "Wesley, you want to step forward? We've got a special prize."

The crowd roared.

I didn't turn around to find out why. I'd seen as much of Wesley Banks as I ever wanted to, and I sure didn't need to watch him hold up a prize for Mr. Petrucelli, like some game show assistant, a big hero just for carrying it into the gym, especially since, whatever it was, it was a prize I'd never win in my whole life, even if I entered the stupid dodgeball tournament, which I never would.

"Each year, everyone wants to be the Last Player Standing," said Mr. Petrucelli.

Earhart Middle whooped and cheered.

"Everyone works hard to be that player," said Mr. Petrucelli, "and usually the only prize is the pride of a job well done. But this year, to commemorate being named Earhart Middle's most valuable player in both football *and* basketball, Wesley, out of his love for school—"

Oh, brother.

"—has generously purchased a prize with his own money, and is donating that prize for the Last Player Standing."

The crowd went wild.

"Wesley will present this prize," said Mr. Petrucelli, "after the championship game at the end of the carnival."

Earhart Middle cheered again.

I shook my head and trundled my spotlight toward the electric plug in the corner. Mom and Beech had wrangled themselves out of the bleachers and were already there waiting for me.

My mother was giving me her sympathetic mom face. Which was just humiliating.

Beech was staring at the middle of the gym, that white, shaky look washed over his face. He kept staring like that, then turned to look at me. And his face just crumpled. Like a Kleenex.

I frowned, glanced over my shoulder . . .

. . . and stopped dead in my combat boots.

Wesley Banks stood in the center of the Amelia M. Earhart Middle School gymnasium, next to Mr. Petrucelli (with the Sundances, Luke Delgado and T.J.

Hawkins, at his side, to make him look even more important, I guess). Just stood there . . .

. . . holding the helmet.

The gold batting helmet, with the red V starting at the top and whooshing back, like Iron Man.

The helmet from Bottenfield's.

The helmet Beecher wanted so much, he was about to pass out.

And as Mr. Petrucelli droned on about how wonderful Wesley was, Wesley did something else entirely. He looked at me. Straight *at* me.

And smiled.

A mean, cold, hard smile.

Nobody else noticed. Mr. Petrucelli was still going on about how amazingly generous Wesley was and how, knowing Wesley and his amazing dodgeball skills, he'd probably end up winning the helmet back anyway, heh heh, and wouldn't that be fitting? The bleacher crowd whooped and clapped. The cheerleaders bounced and cheered. The Kaleys gazed at Wesley like he was a rock star. I don't know what Emma was doing. I couldn't bear to look. But she probably thought Wesley was wonderful too. And then the band director whipped the pep band into a rousing rendition of "He's a Jolly Good Fellow."

And while all this was going on, while everyone

was cheering the thoughtfulness and unselfishness that was Wesley Banks, middle school superhero, Wesley looked at me, then at Beecher, then held the batting helmet high to get the full effect of the gym lights glinting off the shiny red and gold—

—and laughed.

fifteen

To: BassoonMaster
From: SuperTuck
Subject: One Goal

Noah, I finally figured out my New Year's resolution. It will be the greatest thing I will ever achieve, and I'm going to do everything I can, and even some things I probably can't, and not rest a single minute until I make it happen.
Tucker

To: SuperTuck
From: BassoonMaster
Re: One Goal

Tuck, congratulations. So what is it, this perfect resolution?
Noah

To: BassoonMaster
From: SuperTuck
Re: One Goal

I'm going to wipe that stupid, jerky, arrogant smirk off Wesley Banks's face so completely, so thoroughly, no one will ever have to look at it again.
Tucker

To: SuperTuck
From: BassoonMaster
Re: One Goal

I'm in.
Noah

sixteen

I'd never gone to the office to sign up for anything, and sure as heck not an athletic event.

So the next day, between classes, when I ambled into the Amelia M. Earhart Middle School office, trying to act like I knew what I was doing, it was a lie.

Luckily, Louise, our school secretary, spent every day of her life with middle school kids. She had a lot of experience with lies.

She watched for a few moments as I slunk around the office, giving the walls, doors, counter, a covert once-over, hoping the sign-up sheet was maybe taped up somewhere so I could casually add our team and get the heck out of there.

"Hey there, Tucker," she finally said. "What can I do for you?"

"Um, well. I need to sign up for . . . something."

"Would that something be"—she lowered her voice—"Last Player Standing?"

"Yes." I swallowed. "Yes, it would."

Louise gave me a hard look. "Are you sure?"

Was she kidding? I was about to commit a bunch of nervous artists to a cutthroat dodgeball tournament where people like Wesley Banks would fire balls at their heads. And I hadn't told them.

"Yes," I said. "Absolutely."

"Okay, then."

She pulled a clipboard from her desk drawer and carried it to the counter.

"That batting helmet sure is drumming up a lot of interest this year." She licked her fingers and riffled through a stack of papers at the back of the clipboard. "Everybody's sure Wesley will win it back." She gave me a sly wink. "It might be nice if everybody's wrong. Oh, here we are."

She slipped out a sheet of pink paper and handed it to me.

"Your official team roster," she said. "It has to be turned in in a couple weeks."

She set the clipboard on the counter and tapped her fingernail on the top page.

"This is the sign-up sheet. Mr. P. needs an idea of

how many teams we'll have so he can start working on the tournament bracket."

I nodded, shoved the pink paper in my pocket, and pulled the clipboard toward me. A few teams had already signed up. Wesley's team, of course—the Backcourt Bombers. And the wrestling team—Total Takedown. Even the band—Beethoven's Blitz. And one team called the Checkmates. Had to be Chess Club, which gave me hope. I mean, the chess kids were probably less athletic than the art kids, if that was possible.

I took Louise's pen, squared the clipboard on the counter, and scrawled three words.

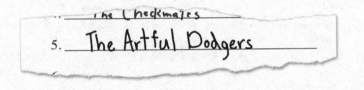

• • •

Coach Wilder paced up and down the aisles of his health classroom, firing off facts about one of his favorite subjects: first aid, or, as he called it, Saving Someone's Life After They've Done Something Stupid.

Everyone else flipped open their health notebooks so they could take notes. I opened my notebook too. Then I dug the pink roster out of my pocket and smoothed it flat against my thigh. I shot a covert look around the room to make sure no one was watching.

For the first time, I realized that all of Art Club was in my health class—Spencer, Martin, Gretchen, Gretchen's friend Olivia who did charcoal drawings and always had black smudges on her face, everyone. Spencer had given me a little wave and a chin lift when I slipped into the room. His chin wouldn't have been nearly as friendly if it knew what it was in for.

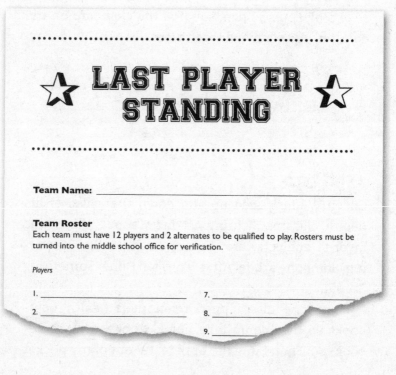

★ **LAST PLAYER STANDING** ★

Team Name: _____

Team Roster
Each team must have 12 players and 2 alternates to be qualified to play. Rosters must be turned into the middle school office for verification.

Players

1. _____   7. _____

2. _____   8. _____

9. _____

I held my pencil over my notebook, like I was probably going to scribble down a note any minute now, and stealthily read the paper in my lap.

Twelve? Plus *alternates?*

I slumped back in my desk chair. I'd thought about a lot of things: Pain. Fear. Art Club's combined physical ability, which equaled zero. But fourteen players? I hadn't thought about *that.*

I was right back where I started: trying to scrounge up new members.

I sighed and slid my finger to the bottom of the page:

Sponsor Signature: _____

That would be the easy part. If I managed to rustle up that many new Art Club members, Mrs. Frazee would be so happy, she'd sign anything.

seventeen

The bell rang. I trudged out of health class, dumped my notebook in my locker, and jostled my way through the packed hall toward Art Club.

Art Club, where we still only had nine members, needed five more in a couple of weeks, and I had no idea where to find them.

I rounded the corner to the electives hallway—

—and got smacked in the face by the bulletin board. The former Art Club bulletin board, which was now plastered with girls' basketball stuff. Team photos. Team rosters. Team articles from the *Wheaton Daily Journal*. And that twangy bent metal piece? No longer a problem. They'd covered it with a tournament bracket so no one could see it.

And they hadn't stopped there.

The bulletin board had sort of exploded with construction paper cutouts—*Win!*, *Rebound!*, *Go, Fighting Aviators!*—blanketing the wall around it. They'd even stuck one right over the light switch *and* the name plaque next to the art room door that said MRS. FRAZEE.

That was just plain rude. How could they think their homemade construction-paper *We're #1* (which was a total lie in the first place) was more important than a safely lit hallway or the name of a highly respected member of our middle school faculty?

It wasn't just rude. It was selfish. It was snotty. It was—it was—*wrong*.

I glanced around. Made sure nobody was watching.

Then slid my fingers under the cutout and popped the tape loose.

I stood there for a minute, paper basketball in my hand, trying not to look like a middle school criminal. I sidled down the hall, found an empty spot on the other side of the bulletin board, and casually pasted the cutout back up.

I stepped back to make sure it looked like it was supposed to be there.

And standing there, gazing at the cutouts and the pictures, I think I actually smiled. The Kaleys would probably screech and rip their whole bulletin board down if they knew this, but they'd just given me an idea.

A great idea.

A genius idea.

An idea that would get us twelve players and two to spare.

When I got home to the Batcave (a.k.a. my bedroom) I unzipped my backpack and slid out the fresh new stack of Bristol board I'd gotten from Mrs. Frazee's Cabinet of Wonders (a.k.a. the art supply closet).

I'd left the Batcave door open, and the blare of the cartoon channel drifted in from the living room.

"Beech?" I hollered.

No reason he couldn't hang out in the Batcave and annoy me for a while if he wanted. I was feeling pumped enough that I could take it.

"Beech?"

No answer. Which I pretty much expected. With the Batmobile blasting through our TV set at approximately ten million decibels, he couldn't hear me even if he wanted to.

And these days, it seemed he didn't much want to.

I swung back around to my desk. Art Club needed members. Members with stamina. Members with agility and accurate throwing arms. Members who would fearlessly enter a dodgeball tournament . . . and win. Members who could beat Wesley Banks and his smirky, smarmy smile.

And I was going to find those members.

Yeah. I know. I'd already given it my best shot, and we saw how *that* turned out. But this was different. This was something I was actually good at. Something I could do.

Something I was born to do.

I sharpened my non-repro blue pencil to a crisp point and started to draw.

eighteen

Noah and I crept down the dimly lit hall. I'd talked him into getting to school early again.

We were here on a covert ops mission. Packed in our arsenal: one comic book page, one heavy winter coat, one roll of Scotch tape.

We rounded the corner past the electives hall and stopped outside the lunchroom. I glanced around to make sure the hall was empty, then pulled my Beanboy page from its waterproof carrying case.

I'd chosen the location carefully. Earhart middle-schoolers packed into this hallway every day at noon, forming a disorganized line leading into the cafeteria. As they inched along, they'd have plenty of time to read the latest adventures of Beanboy.

Yes, "adventures." Plural. This page was only the first.

Noah pulled off his gloves. "Approximately three hundred students attend Earhart Middle. Of those students, roughly one third participate in athletics, and another third in assorted clubs and academic teams. That leaves fully one third of the Earhart population—one hundred students—unassociated with any organized, school-related activity. Out of those, you only need five. Five of the one hundred remaining available students. That's five percent."

I could always count on Noah for an encouraging statistic.

I held my Beanboy page against the wall. As Earhart Middle moved through the lunch line, stomachs growling, they'd spot it. And read it. At first they'd probably wonder what it was and who put it up.

But a couple days later, they'd see another page, and another, till pretty soon they were caught up in Beanboy's adventures. Every day at noon, they'd bolt for the cafeteria, but they wouldn't be coming for the tater tots. They'd be coming to see what happened next. They'd want to know what impossible situation Madame Fury had put Beanboy in this time, and what cool thing Beanboy would do to escape. They'd want to see how the Art Club at Beanboy's (a.k.a. Austin

Peabody's) high school would use their ingenious art tricks to help him.

And maybe they'd think Art Club could help them too. Maybe they'd want to be part of it.

Hopefully, people with physical agility and accurate throwing arms.

I held my Beanboy page in one hand, the roll of tape in the other. Noah casually moved in front of me. He unzipped his coat and made a big show of taking it off, his arms spread wide, hiding me behind it just in case one of the lunch ladies peeked out from the kitchen or the janitor rumbled past with her mop bucket.

(Although we could probably dodge the janitor without much trouble right now. She'd been hobbling around with a brace on her knee since winter break. We thought it was maybe something glamorous and exciting, like a skiing accident, but she said she slipped while she was trying to scrape ice off her car.)

I tore off a piece of Scotch tape and fixed my Beanboy page to the wall.

The bell rang for lunch. I bolted from math class into the mob of middle-schoolers. They talked, laughed, and crowded toward the cafeteria. I kept my head down and squeezed my way through.

Noah caught up with me outside the lunchroom. We were near the end of the line. I stretched, trying to see over the crowd, carefully counting the number of fellow Earhart students who stopped to read my comic book page.

It was easy to keep track of: zero. Not one person was gazing at the wall, stunned by the sheer awesomeness that was Beanboy.

"I wouldn't be too concerned," said Noah. "By the time lunch rolls around, people are starving. Too wiped out to read anything on a wall. Look—Gunnar Shoemaker's nibbling his lunch card, and Martin Higby looks like he's about to pass out from sheer hunger. But don't worry. Eventually somebody'll notice. Maybe this afternoon or tomorrow or something. And they'll show their friends, and they'll show *their* friends. It'll catch on."

I nodded. I hoped he was right.

We finally inched close enough so I could see the spot where I'd taped Beanboy.

Nobody was reading it.

Nobody was *ever* going to read it.

They couldn't.

My comic book page was gone.

nineteen

Do you ever feel like the universe is working against you? Like no matter how hard you try, no matter how many genius ideas you come up with, no matter what you do to become a more respectable human being, the universe is never going to let it happen?

The next morning, Noah heaved open the thick metal door and we shuffled into Earhart Middle. The door clanked shut behind us. We stood there for a second in the sudden warmth to let Noah's glasses unfog. I wiped my shoes on the big entry mat.

And found myself, once again, watching Wesley Banks. I didn't mean to. But he was taller than everybody (well, *almost* everybody—Dillon Zawicki was taller, but Dillon spent so much time in detention, he wasn't around to be tall very often), so even in a crowded hallway, Wesley wasn't hard to spot. The whole boys' basketball team was clotted around him—even guys who hardly ever played, like Owen Skeet and his buddy Curtis—apparently fascinated by the way he shoved his backpack into his locker.

I shook my head. Wesley Banks, supervillain in disguise, could be a rock star just by standing in a hallway.

I peeled off my gloves and shoved them in my coat pockets.

I'd spent yesterday afternoon hunting for my Beanboy page. I looked up and down the hall and under the tables in the cafeteria, in case it had torn loose and floated into some forgotten corner somewhere.

It hadn't.

I tracked down the janitor's cart to see if maybe when she'd dragged her industrial-size dust mop through the cafeteria after lunch, sweeping up used napkins and dirt, she'd accidentally swept my page up, too.

She hadn't.

I even picked through the garbage in the big trash bins in the lunchroom. Not my proudest moment. I found lots of beans. Cold, dead, boiled-to-mush green beans, scraped from lunch trays and clinging to crumpled milk cartons like an invasion of limp larvae.

But no Beanboy. My genius idea was just . . . gone.

The door banged open behind us and a clump of fellow middle school students barreled in. Noah and I scuttled off to the side to keep from being mowed down.

The clump giggled its way down the hallway. One of the girls stopped, tugged on her friend's coat sleeve, and pointed at something on a locker. The whole clump stopped and stared. Moved in for a closer look.

For a minute I couldn't move. A chill snaked through me.

"Noah," I whispered. "Look."

Noah squinted. "What—how—?"

I shook my head. "No clue."

Because up and down the hallway, in both directions, taped to lockers, walls, doors, bulletin boards, the windows of the middle school office, the janitor's closet, were copy after copy of . . .

. . . my Beanboy page.

The page I'd stuck up by the cafeteria. The page nobody had gotten a chance to see.

Now they were seeing. Not everyone. Most people were digging books out of their lockers and rubbing sleep crust from their eyes and scrambling toward first hour so they wouldn't be late.

But a few clumps of students, here and there, had stopped to look.

Which was kind of cool. Exactly what I'd wanted.

But also kind of disturbing. Now that people were

actually looking at my page, actually reading it, well, it was like I'd accidentally shown up at school naked and it was too late to go back and put on pants.

I hiked up my backpack, Noah hiked up his bassoon case, and we plunged into the crowded hallway. As we jostled our way toward our lockers, I cast stealth glances at the clumps reading my comic book page, and it seemed like they actually . . . didn't hate it.

My ears perked to pick up random comments:

"Wow. They're everywhere."

"I wonder who did it."

"I never thought about it, but saving the world *would* be pretty exhausting."

And then the one I really liked:

"Where's the rest of the story?"

Someone wanted more. At least one person wanted to read more.

And then the one I liked best, from Owen Skeet, a quiet, lanky kid. He stared at my page, his face wrinkled into a thoughtful frown.

"Invisible," Owen mumbled to himself. "Yeah."

twenty

As Noah says, middle school attention spans are frustratingly short. By the time the bell rang for first hour, everyone seemed to have forgotten all about my comic book page.

Then I ambled into Art Club after school ... and was hit by a mob.

"Dude! Genius!"

Spencer tried to give me a chest bump and got his new knitted scarf (Great-Aunt Bernice had been busy again) caught in the strap of my backpack.

"Nobody expected *that*," he said as he untangled himself. "We were all pretty glum about the whole pep assembly incident, but you—you thought of a whole *new* way to get people interested. Awesome!"

Gretchen Klamm nodded. "Completely."

"I couldn't believe it." Martin Higby shook his head. "Copies were everywhere!"

"Who needs a bulletin board when you can use the whole school?"

"Excellent idea!"

Their compliments draped over me, warm and fluffy like a blanket.

Except, said a pesky voice in my head, *you don't deserve it.*

The pesky voice had a point. Yeah, I'd drawn the comic book page. But I sure hadn't been the one who plastered the school with it. Plus, while Art Club was all "Awesome!" "Excellent!" about my new plan, I didn't mention the other part, the part where I lined them up in the gym so bigger, stronger kids (a.k.a. Wesley Banks) could hurl dodgeballs at them.

Mrs. Frazee gave my shoulder a squeeze. "You've really embraced performance art, Tucker. You've turned it into a true event, become part of it—a secret artist, bringing his artwork to the people like a phantom in the night." She clapped her hands together in pure art-teacher delight. "Zorro with a copy machine."

I blinked. Zorro with a copy machine. I liked it.

"I just want you to know"—she leaned in, her voice low—"I spoke to Mr. Petrucelli about it this morning."

Oh, man. Mr. Petrucelli. I hadn't even thought about *him*.

"I pointed out the many signs and posters we put up for other clubs and teams," said Mrs. Frazee. "I let him know that this comic book page is part of our Art Club activities."

Wow. Mrs. Frazee had my back.

Not just yours, said my pesky voice. *While you're standing there listening to how awesome you are and letting your head swell up like a dead fish, don't forget: Someone in this room knows the truth.*

Another good point. One that had been gnawing on my brain all day. As Mrs. Frazee handed out the face paints and brushes we'd need for our booth at the school carnival, I watched the Art Club members, who cheerfully snatched them up.

One of them had to be the Phantom Photocopier. *Had* to be. Who else would care if anyone saw my comic book pages?

Not the Kaleys. Not Wesley Banks or the Sundances. And sure as heck not Mr. Petrucelli.

Nobody.

Except Art Club.

"So." Spencer sidled up to me. He peeked over his shoulder. "We took a vote and it was unanimous. Nobody in Art Club will reveal your true identity as the comic book artist."

I eyed him. Was it Spencer? Was all that "Dude! Genius!" stuff just a big cover for his own clandestine activities?

"So." He hiked up his jeans. "When are you putting up another one? I mean, you *are* putting up another one, right?"

No. I couldn't picture it. I couldn't picture Spencer Osterholtz—with his knitted cap and his gangly, stumbling feet—stealing through Earhart Middle, taping up comic book pages without anyone noticing.

He was looking at me, expecting an answer.

"Well," I said, "I'm still working on it. I want it to be a . . . surprise."

twenty-one

When I popped out onto Polk Street, I found Sam and Beecher lying in the yard.

Sam had bundled Beech into his winter coat, gloves, and boots, his hood tied tight, his scarf wound around his neck all the way up to his nose so the only part you could see of him were his two eyes blinking out from behind all that bundling.

Sam was zipped tight, too, and the two of them were sprawled on their backs in the snow, beside Joe and Samir's shoveled piles, flapping their arms and legs.

Making snow angels.

Which was really weird since snow totally freaks Beecher out (he's terrified he'll slip and fall) and since an angel was maybe the last thing on the planet I thought Sam Zawicki would ever want to make.

But there she was, sliding her arms and legs and laughing about it with Beech, her giggles puffing out in little white clouds above her.

Beecher's voice floated across the snow. "Tell Mrs. Hottins," he said.

"Your teacher?" said Sam.

"Tell her we do angels."

I made my way up the front walk.

"So . . . hey," I said.

Sam stopped flapping and sat up. She pushed the sleeve of her parka up to check her watch.

"Crud," she muttered.

She carefully stood and leaped across the snow, to keep from messing up her snow angel with footprints, I guess. She leaned down and helped Beech up too. Lifted him out so his angel wouldn't get messed up either.

She set him down on the walk and grabbed her satchel off the porch step.

Then she stopped. She studied Beecher's snow angel.

"Does he need a cape?" she asked him.

Beech shook his head. "Not superhero."

"You sure? He looks like a superhero."

Beech shook his head again. "Not superhero."

Sam let out a breath. "Okay."

She hoisted the satchel onto her shoulder and bolted off down the walk. About knocked me into Joe and Samir's shoveled piles.

"Glad to see you too," I said as I swirled my arms to regain my balance.

Beech and I watched as she disappeared down Polk Street.

I shook my head. Who knew what was up with her lately? I mean, first she goes all grizzly bear defending the bulletin board, and after that it was like she couldn't stand being on the same planet as me.

I crouched over my desk in the Batcave—a stealth comic book genius hunkered down in his secret hideaway. I gripped my pencil. Steadied my hand. Took aim at my sheet of Bristol board. And drew . . .

. . . nothing.

I sank back in my desk chair.

I let out a sigh.

I couldn't draw. My brain wouldn't let me.

I pulled my health notebook from my backpack, turned to an empty page, and scribbled out a list.

I stared out the window. It had to be someone in Art Club. But who? Not Spencer. He had the enthusiasm, for sure. But the skills? No.

Plus, if Spencer had done it, all the photocopies would have little knitted picture frames.

So who? I sifted through the members of Art Club in my head.

Gretchen Klamm? Too timid.

Martin Higby? Too disorganized.

So who?

Who could get into the school when nobody else was there? Who could plaster the halls with copies? Who could *make* all those copies in the first place?

I stopped.

One person could do all that without anyone noticing, not even Mr. Petrucelli. I studied my list again.

Things I Know For Sure About
The Phantom Photocopier

1. Likes Art Club

2. Is pretty sneaky

3. Has a Xerox machine and knows how to use it

4. ?

I gripped my pencil and scribbled the name across the middle of the page.

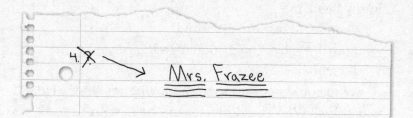

Tucker MacBean's Top Secret Undercover
Beanboy Comic Book Page #2:

twenty-two

Noah and I crept through the early-morning gray of the hallway, comic book page, winter coat, and Scotch tape at the ready.

When we reached the hall outside the lunchroom, I whipped out the page, Noah wrangled his coat in the air for cover, and I taped the page to the wall.

When the lunch bell rang, I darted from math class, made my way toward the lunchroom, and stretched to get a better view of the wall.

Once again, it was empty.

But this time, I didn't trudge into the lunchroom, cursing the universe.

This time I did a little fist pump.

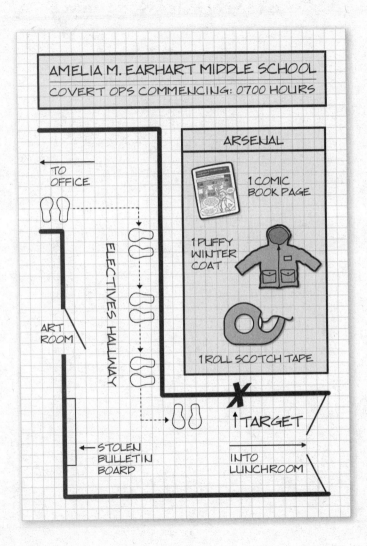

AMELIA M. EARHART MIDDLE SCHOOL

COVERT OPS COMMENCING: 0700 HOURS

ARSENAL

1 COMIC BOOK PAGE

1 PUFFY WINTER COAT

1 ROLL SCOTCH TAPE

TO OFFICE

ELECTIVES HALLWAY

ART ROOM

TARGET

STOLEN BULLETIN BOARD

INTO LUNCHROOM

All that remained
of my Beanboy page

twenty-three

The next morning, Noah and I heaved open the thick metal door and stepped into Earhart Middle.

And saw approximately six gazillion copies of my comic book page plastered up and down the halls of Amelia M. Earhart Middle School.

And clumps of fellow Earhart students, here and there, reading them.

Noah wiped his mitten over his glasses.

"I believe," he said in a low voice, "that this time there are even more."

I peered down the hallway. Copies of Beanboy taped on every vertical surface—lockers, walls, doors, windows. "More pages?"

"No," he said. "More people."

He was right. The clumps of Earhart middle-schoolers reading my page had grown. And multiplied. That weird naked feeling started to creep over me again.

Noah hiked up his bassoon, I hiked up my book-bag, and we pushed our way down the crowded hallway, ears tuned to pick up what the clumps were saying:

"Hey, look. It's another one."

"This mad scientist lady must be the bad guy."

"*Really* bad if she doesn't want kids to be happy."

"I wonder what she's going to do next."

Noah and I thumped each other a covert fist bump. Earhart Middle was starting to catch on.

And not just the students. Standing in the middle of the hall, kids darting around him like a river flowing around a big stuck log, was Coach Wilder, squinting at a Beanboy page and rubbing a big sausage hand over his bristly chin.

When I walked into the art room that day after school, I was greeted by a drawing on the chalkboard:

Spencer scuttled over to greet me. He hitched up his jeans. His chalky fingers left long white marks on his legs.

"That was my idea." He tipped his head toward the chalkboard. His stocking cap puffed with pride. "I mean, it was your idea originally, of course, but it was my idea to get here early and write it in big letters. Mrs. Frazee says we can keep it there. You know, for motivation."

"Wow," I said. "That's just—wow."

And it was. Art Club had always been smart. No question. But now, as Art Club members drifted into the room, talking and laughing, their own faces were, well, *bright*, and I realized they also seemed happier lately. And yeah, more self-confident.

Art Club really *was* the home of happy, self-confident, smart people.

Sure, muttered my pesky voice. *They're happy now. But you haven't told them about the dodgeball tournament.*

"I will. I'm *going* to," I muttered back. "When we get enough people."

Spencer gave me a weird look. "What?"

"Oh—nothing," I said. "My stomach's just grumbling. I think I got a bad corn dog at lunch."

"I hear you." Spencer nodded sympathetically. "Deep-fried meat can be a killer."

I nodded too. But as I glanced around the room

at my fellow Art Club members, happily practicing their face-painting technique for the school carnival, I realized it was still just us. Just the nine of us. My Beanboy pages had been drumming up interest up and down the hallways, and they'd given Art Club a confident glow, but they still weren't doing what I truly needed them to do: suck in new members.

I needed to bump up my game.

Tucker MacBean's Top Secret Undercover Beanboy Comic Book Page #3:

twenty-four

By now I pretty much knew what to expect: Noah and I would arrive at school, lug ourselves through the front door, stand inside on the big mat while Noah wiped his glasses and I wiped my feet, and then Noah would hoist his bassoon, I'd hoist my backpack, and we'd pick our way through ever-growing clumps of kids reading the comic book pages that had been magically plastered up and down the hall overnight by the Phantom Photocopier.

I sure didn't expect what we saw *this* morning.

My pages were there. And clumps of kids were standing and staring.

But they weren't staring at Beanboy.

They were staring at the ceiling.

Hanging from the ceiling in the front hallway of

Amelia M. Earhart Middle School, from corner to corner and side to side, over the lockers, above the lights, atop the trophy case, were T-shirts, hoodies, random socks, gloves, hats, a scarf or two, some backpacks, spiral notebooks, broken pencils, stray homework, crumpled lunch bags, earbuds, gym shorts, gym shoes—all tied together and draped above our heads like a string of Christmas lights.

I pointed to a grubby scrap of springy fabric dangling over the office door. "Is that a—"

"Jockstrap?" Noah nodded. "Yes. Yes, it is."

Noah and I plowed through the crowd. About plowed smack into Mr. Petrucelli.

He was standing outside the middle school office, his serious principal hands planted on his hips, his serious principal lips pooched out in deep concentration. He gazed up the hall in one direction, scrutinized the string of draped stuff, then turned and gazed the other way.

Mr. Petrucelli must've seen all he needed to see, because he shook his head, turned on his serious principal heel, and clicked back into the office. The door rattled shut behind him.

That's when I noticed Owen Skeet. Again. He was standing on the other side of the office. And he was maybe the only kid in Earhart Middle not staring at the dangling jockstrap.

Owen Skeet was reading my Beanboy page. And

nodding. He pulled his gawky body up to its full height, which was actually pretty tall once he wasn't slumped over, squared his usually hunched shoulders, and headed off down the hall.

"Good morning, Amelia M. Earhart Middle School students." The intercom crackled to life. Mr. Petrucelli's voice blared through first-hour social studies.

"As I'm sure you all know, the school has been experiencing instances of, well, not vandalism precisely. Let's call it inappropriate repositioning of property. In other words, someone has been hanging shoes, school supplies, clothing, and other items from lights, doorways, and other inappropriate places. I only hope these incidents aren't connected in any way to the, uh, comic book pages that I've allowed to be placed in our hallways."

Comic book pages? I nearly dropped my pencil.

Noah sat right in front of me. He turned around and gave me a horrified look.

"I haven't said anything up to this point," Mr. Petrucelli continued, "because the incidents have been small, and I was willing to overlook minor transgressions. But as I'm sure you are all aware, this inappropriate repositioning has recently escalated to a level that is distracting and interferes with student learning. To the person or persons responsible, this serves as a warning: if these inappropriate incidents do not cease immediately, you will face *very* appropriate consequences."

The intercom went dead and we all thought he was done. Students shuffled their notebooks and shifted in their seats. Mr. Luzensky scratched his head and tried to find his place in our social studies book.

The intercom buzzed back to life.

"If anyone is missing a pair of gym shorts or, ah, other items, please see Louise in the office. Thank you."

Case File:
Mr. P

Status: I'll probably get permanent dentention for even thinking it, but I gotta go with my gut (and personal experience) on this one: SUPERVILLAIN. Yeah. I said it.

Base: Amelia M. Earhart Middle School office.

Superpower: Teleportation. Has to be. The guy is everywhere, especially everywhere you don't want him to be.

Superweapon: Serious principal eyeballs that focus like a laser, never flinching, never wavering, drilling into your skull until before you know what's happening, you're spilling your guts about everything you have ever done wrong in your life and some things that weren't wrong because suddenly you can't stop yourself.

Real Name: Vincent G. Petrucelli, Middle School Principal

twenty-five

Art Club was turning into a new surprise every day.

Today Spencer was waiting for me inside the door.

"Your comic book's working." His voice was a whisper. "We recruited a new member."

"Really?"

I thought about this. Owen Skeet *had* been reading my Beanboy page that morning. Owen wasn't the first person who came to mind when you thought about ferocious athletes, but he *was* on the basketball team. Mostly he rode the bench. But still, this was a person who could throw a ball. And catch it without falling down. Usually. Owen Skeet was something the Amelia M. Earhart Middle School art room had never seen before. Owen Skeet was . . .

. . . an athlete.

"Where?" I said.

Spencer motioned his stocking cap toward the corner.

I turned. And stared at the heap of a person slouched at my desk, stretched out over it sideways, his beefy head propped up in one beefy palm.

Owen didn't have beefy palms. Owen didn't have beefy anything. This person looked exactly like . . .

Dillon.

Zawicki. I swallowed. Dillon Zawicki was stretched all over my tilty-topped art desk. The universe was just messing with me now.

Dillon caught me looking at him. He shrugged one lump of a shoulder. "Sam said I had to."

Case File: Dillon

(That's it. Just Dillon. It's kind of like Elvis. You just have to say his first name and everyone knows who you mean.)

Status: If you ask Sam, she'd say he's a sidekick. Hers. Even though she doesn't claim him half the time, and lately not at all. If you ask anyone else at Earhart Middle, he's a supervillain. Definitely.

Base: Patrolling the Earhart Middle School hallways.

Superpower: Super strength.

Superweapon: Great hulking size. I'm sure there's more to it than that, but since his upper arms are as big around as basketballs, nobody's ever been brave enough to find out.

Real Name: Dillon Zawicki

I nodded.

Spencer leaned toward me. "This is good, right? I mean, we need new members and there's"—he waved a nervous hand toward Dillon—"a new member. So that's progress. Right?"

"Maybe," I said. "I need to give it some thought."

I caught movement out of the corner of my eye and turned to see someone lurking in the art room doorway.

This time it *was* Owen Skeet, middle school athlete.

As he hovered there, shoulders hunched, long skinny arms hanging down like he wasn't sure where to put them, shaggy hair drooping over his eyes, and all of Art Club gawking, Owen looked like a trapped animal, a specimen we'd caught and brought back to the lab to study.

His gaze darted around the room.

And landed on Dillon, who was still stretched out on my desk, taking a nap, it looked like.

Owen's arms stiffened. His shaggy hair about stood on end.

"Oh. Uh." He took a step backwards. "Wrong door. I thought this was the, um, bathroom. Sorry."

He turned and shot down the hall.

twenty-six

I slipped out of Art Club early, raced home, and tip-toed up the stairs to the MacBean Family Apartment—quietly, so I could take Sam by surprise and maybe catch her before she could stomp out.

I carefully turned the knob and pushed the kitchen door open.

There was Sam, leaning against the counter, arms crossed, watching the clock on the microwave. Parka zipped and snapped. Satchel already swung over her shoulder.

The minute she saw me, she pushed off the counter and gave Beecher's hair a ruffle.

"See you, kid," she said.

"Oh!" I blinked. "So—"

She pushed past me.

"—I just wanted to ask—"

She thundered out of the apartment.

"—why you made Dillon—"

The door slammed shut in my face. (One of these days she was going to bang it right off its hinges.)

"—join Art Club," I said to the door.

Beech had been sitting at the table with a slice of peanut butter toast, with raisins poked into the peanut butter for a face, turning it one way and another, trying to figure out the best place to take a bite without hurting it.

Now he let out a sympathetic sigh. "Tupid thing again."

I didn't have time to decipher whatever Sam and Beech had been talking about. I wrenched the door open and bolted out after her.

I caught her at the bottom of the stairs. She whirled on me, practically breathing fire, one fist gripping the doorknob, the other clenched tight at her side.

"So, hey," I said, in a completely friendly voice. I propped my elbow on the banister, like I'd just come down to chat. "Dillon's in Art Club now, huh?"

That was it, I swear. That's all I said.

She narrowed her eyes. "What, you think Dillon's not good enough for your club?"

"What?" I stared at her. "No. I didn't—that's not what I—"

Man. Ask one little innocent question and this is what I get: blasted by a fire-breathing babysitter.

"I thought you *wanted* more people in Art Club," she said.

"Well . . . yeah—"

"So maybe you should thank me."

This was not going the way I planned. What I'd planned was that

1. I would say—in a completely casual way— "So hey, Dillon's in Art Club," and then
2. Sam—also completely casual—would divulge information, like *why* Dillon was in Art Club all of a sudden.

It was as if my plan had never met Sam Zawicki.

She twisted the knob and wrenched the front door open. She put her head down to push her way out into the wind.

Then she turned back, eyes narrowed, chin jutted out.

"Why *can't* Dillon be in your club?" she said.

"He can. He is. Nobody said—"

"Because he's got just as much business there as anybody. And he's got to be *somewhere*. I can't watch him all the time. It's okay in the mornings, but I can't be there after school because I'm *here* every day, and

Dillon can't just go around"—she flung a hand in the air—"unsupervised."

Boy, *that* was sure true.

But I was still confused.

"Isn't your grandpa there?" I said.

She pressed her lips into a narrow line. "Grandpa's busy," she said.

"Oh."

I was no expert, but I'd always thought January in Kansas was probably the *not*-busy time for farmers. They even closed the farmers' market downtown during the winter, and that's where Sam's grandpa sold his beets and potatoes and apples and stuff.

"So vegetables grow this time of year?" I said.

(And again, I need to point out that I was being completely friendly and conversational.)

Sam speared me with a glare. "No, vegetables do not grow this time of year. It's freezing. What is wrong with you?"

I blew out a breath. "I don't *know* what's wrong with me. Something serious, I guess, because I actually thought maybe if I asked nice, you'd be nice back and tell me what was up. And I *was* going to thank you, because Art Club needs all the people it can get. So thank you for giving us Dillon. Also, I was going to ask you if there's anything he especially wants to do in Art Club since he won't talk to any of us, including Mrs. Frazee."

I turned and marched back upstairs, the old wooden steps squeaking beneath my sneakers.

Sam's growl drifted up behind me. "He's already had six detentions this year."

I stopped and turned around.

She pushed the front door shut, blocking out the winter.

"Six." She crossed her arms over her army jacket. "You know what that means?"

I looked at her. How would I know what that meant?

"Um, no," I said.

Sam stared up at me. "Don't you read your student handbook?"

"Do *you?*"

She shook her head. "That whole thing last year with Dillon and the missing milk forced me to read it."

Sam blew out a breath. By this time her rage had deflated, and she'd deflated along with it. She stood there, her back against our front door.

"He's the one who hung all that stuff up," she said. "You know, in Mr. Petrucelli's announcement? Dillon found gym shorts and shoes all over the locker room, and other stuff just left all over the school, so he took them and strung them up in the hall. To teach people a lesson. So next time they'd pick their stuff up and not leave such a mess."

Such a mess? I stopped for a minute to let this sink in.

Dillon never even bothered to tie his mud-crusted size-sixteen sneakers. Just ambled along with his shoelaces dragging through the floor grit. And also, when he turned in his homework—*if* he turned in his homework—it was always a grubby gray mess from all the smears and eraser marks and general grime.

"He thinks he's defending Grandpa," said Sam.

I frowned. "Against gym shorts?"

Sam studied me for a long minute, till it felt like she was studying a hole right through me.

"The janitor messed up her knee," she said finally. "And that big storm last fall flattened everything Grandpa was growing. We needed *something,* so Grandpa got a job before and after school, helping the janitor till her knee's better."

"Oh. That makes sense."

She shook her head. "It'd make better sense if Dillon would wind down. One morning he found a desk one of the teachers had scooted out into the hallway and forgot to scoot back. Lucky I was there to stop him before he shoved it up on top of the trophy case. He says Grandpa's job's hard enough already and he doesn't need extra work."

I thought about this, about Sam's grandpa, a really nice white-haired man with arms as tough as rope from all that farming, and with boots so worn out he had to duct-tape them together, a man who always made the extra effort to squat down and talk to Beecher face to face every time we showed up at the farmers' market, even though his work-worn knees crackled in protest all the way down and all the way back up again.

I couldn't believe I was actually about to agree with Dillon Zawicki, but suddenly there I was, with these words coming out of my mouth: "He has a point."

Sam shot me a sharp, surprised look. "Yeah. But do you think he could do something useful with it? Like, I don't know, *help?* No. He just makes life harder for everybody, mostly for Grandpa, but also for me, because I'm the one who has to worry about what he's doing when I'm not there to stop him. Dillon could get kicked out of school, and Grandpa could lose his job. They find out about Dillon, they'll think my grandpa's an accomplice."

"Well, now that Dillon's in Art Club," I said, "maybe he won't have time to get your grandpa fired. Plus that'll give us one more person, even if he never talks to us." I gave her a shaky thumbs-up. "Win-win."

She looked at me, to make sure I wasn't kidding.

"Okay then," she said.

"Okay then," I said.

She turned the doorknob. "You tell anybody *any* of this, Beanboy, you will be sorrier than you've ever been in your entire miserable life."

I nodded. "Understood."

twenty-seven

When Noah and I arrived at school in the gray early-morning hours, we didn't figure this time would be any different from any of the others.

After we taped up my Beanboy page, we swung back around to the electives hallway, passed the completely annoying girls' basketball display sprawled all over our stolen bulletin board, started past the art room, and saw a sheet stuck to the art room door.

I stopped. Put it in reverse. Peered at the paper.

Canceled? Spots floated before my eyes.

"It's happening," I managed to choke out. "Just like the yearbook said it would."

Through the floating spots, I saw Noah crinkle his face into a frown.

ATTENTION:

Art Club has been canceled until further notice.

Mrs. Frazee has the flu and will not be here today. Art Club will resume after she returns. Thank you.

"What are you talking about?" He poked a finger at the bottom of the sheet, to the rest of the note written in smaller letters.

Mrs. Frazee has the flu and will not be here today.
Art Club will resume when she returns.
Thank you.

"Oh." I sagged in relief. "Mrs. Frazee's just sick. That's good."

Noah shook his head. "The flu's nothing to mess with. I'm sure Mrs. Frazee feels like roadkill about now."

I was a horrible person. I hadn't even thought about poor Mrs. Frazee, lying in her sick bed, feverish and miserable, too sick to drag herself to school, until Noah pointed it out.

I hadn't thought about Mrs. Frazee because I was thinking about my Beanboy page, about what would happen if she wasn't there to copy and tape it, and then I was also trying to figure out how long it took a person to get over the flu and back to copying and taping.

I hoped Mrs. Frazee never found out.

But at lunchtime, as Noah and I inched our way through the line outside the cafeteria, I stared at the wall.

It was gone.

My Beanboy page was gone.

I tried not to get my hopes up, but when Noah and I ambled into Earhart Middle the next morning and stopped inside the door to unfog and thaw, I sneaked a peak down the hall.

And there, among the morning rumble and chaos of the Amelia M. Earhart Middle School hallway, were approximately three zillion copies of my Beanboy page, taped to walls and doors, lockers and windows.

Mrs. Frazee was home sick with the flu. But the Phantom Photocopier copied on.

One voice, shiny and clear, floated above the rumble of the hall: "I don't know who's drawing these, but whoever it is, he's pretty cool."

I stopped dead.

I'd finally heard it, the word nobody had ever used to describe me before.

Cool.

And the person who said it?

Emma Quinn.

twenty-eight

Emma Quinn thought I was cool.

I dumped my health book on my desk and slapped my notebook down beside it.

The shiniest girl in all of Wheaton thought I was cool.

Well, not me particularly.

Not Tucker MacBean, Real Live Person.

But Tucker MacBean, Comic Book Genius.

"So. Have you told them yet?"

I looked up, startled.

Noah was already settled into his seat in front of me. He positioned his health book on the scarred desktop, then placed his notebook, pencil, and eraser in a parallel row beside it.

He turned around. Raised a questioning eyebrow.

I shook my head. "Not yet."

"You're running out of time."

"I know. I have a plan."

He kept looking at me.

"I *do*." I scooted into my seat. "Really."

I did have a plan. Squarely tucked in my shoe. I'd worked on it all through social studies and put the final touches on during math.

You may have noticed I'm not very good with words. In person, anyway. When I'm drawing a comic book, the words come out perfect. My superheroes know exactly what to say. They have speech bubbles above their heads that take care of it for them. If I, Tucker MacBean, Real Live Person, could walk around with a speech bubble over my head, I'd know what to say too.

Four score and seven years ago, our fathers brought forth on this continent a new tournament, conceived for the school carnival and dedicated to the proposition that all students should be pummeled with dodgeballs equally...

I might even know how to tell Art Club that—*sur-prise!*—they were dodgeball players.

Coach Wilder rubbed his hands together, clearly psyched about the fascinating health topic of the day: abrasions, or as he called it, When Knees Become Hamburger.

I flipped to a clean page in my health notebook.

"Anybody going out for track this spring?" Coach Wilder paced around the health room. "Thinking about running hurdles?" He gazed over the sea of middle-schoolers and gave a knowing nod. "You'll find out about hamburger pretty quick."

Coach Wilder began spouting abrasion facts and figures. Around me, fellow Earhart students sighed, propped their heads on their hands, and began scratching notes, trying their best not to lapse into a coma from sheer boredom.

(Except Noah, of course. He was sitting straight as a stick, logging every health fact in faithful detail and, knowing Noah, adding a few facts of his own, facts he would thoughtfully share with Coach Wilder later.)

The other Art Club members kept themselves awake by drawing sketches and doodles or, in Spencer's case, new knitwear designs for Great-Aunt Bernice.

"Step one"—Coach Wilder held up one sausage of a finger—"clean the wound. Step two—"

A sharp rap echoed through the room.

Coach Wilder glanced up. All of health class turned to stare at the back of the room.

The door rattled open, and there, slouched in the doorway, was Wesley Banks—the office aide this hour.

He swaggered into the room. "Sorry to interrupt." He cocked his chin at Coach Wilder, like he knew that wherever he went, whatever he did, it was never an interruption. "Official business."

He held up a sheet of paper. A sheet of pink paper. A sheet of paper that looked frighteningly familiar.

I closed my eyes. This couldn't be good.

"Oh, hey, there you are . . . *Tut*."

Wesley locked his gaze on me. His face hardened

into a cold, hard smirk. He strutted down the aisle and stopped in front of my desk.

"Mr. P told me to give you this." He waved the pink sheet in my face. "In case you lost the first one."

"Uh, thanks," I managed to say.

I reached for the paper, hoping to slip it under my health notebook before anyone saw what it was.

But Wesley pulled it away. He held it out of my reach.

"Now, now, now, Tut," he said. "Let's not get grabby."

Martin Higby sat in the row beside me. Wesley settled himself on the edge of Martin's desk, crushing the pages of Martin's health book. He stretched his legs into the aisle, one jumbo basketball shoe crossed over the other, his arms folded across his chest, the pink paper still clutched in his hand.

"I take my office aide duties seriously," he said. "Mr. P gave me a message, and I promised I'd make sure you got it. This roster"—he gave it a rustle—"has to be turned in by the end of the period."

End of the period?

"But I thought—" I swallowed. "I mean, Louise said—"

"I don't know anything about Louise." Wesley gave a fake innocent shrug. "All I know is what Mr. P told me. He's working on the bracket, and if he doesn't get your roster, well"—he gave a fake sympathetic shake of his head—"you and your little art friends won't be able to play dodgeball."

At the words "art friends," all of Art Club snapped to attention. Their eyes—wide and unblinking—drilled into me.

twenty-nine

"Dodgeball?"

Art Club stared at me in horror.

Everyone else poked one another and laughed.

The Kaleys rolled their eyes and shot each other a loser dweeb look, a look that clearly said, "You have *got* to be kidding me. The loser dweebs are out of control. *Now* they think they can play *dodgeball*."

I stared at the back of Noah's seat, my cheeks so hot, I was sure they had spontaneously burst into flames while I was sitting there. I wanted to touch them just to be sure, but I didn't want to draw attention in case somebody in the room hadn't noticed. Out of the corner of my eye, I could see Wesley's smile turn even smirkier.

Sometimes I wish I had a secret button on my

backpack that I could press and wherever I was, a concealed passage would open beneath my feet. The floor would slide apart, I'd drop down out of sight, the floor would slide shut again, and I could make my escape without anyone looking at me. Noah could probably invent something like that. I needed to get him on it. While he was at it, maybe he could invent a time machine, too, so I could just erase this whole day. Or week. Or heck, everything back to Christmas. Before Bottenfield's and the batting helmet and the bulletin board, before I'd hatched my brilliant dodge-ball scheme.

"Thank you, Banks."

I looked up. While everyone had been busy staring at me, Coach Wilder had ambled down the aisle. Now he ripped the pink roster from Wesley's grip.

"I think we can take it from here," he said.

"No problem, Coach." Wesley casually hefted himself from Martin's desk. "Just doing my job."

He swaggered toward the door.

Coach Wilder handed the roster to me.

"Thanks," I mumbled.

I slid it under my health notebook. Picked up my pencil and held it at the ready, like I couldn't wait to get back to the fascinating topic of abrasions. I hoped my flaming hot cheeks would put themselves out pretty soon.

As Wesley's jumbo basketball shoes thudded toward the door, Coach Wilder revved up again.

"Step one"—he again held up one sausage finger—"clean the wound. Step two—"

"You really think we can play in the tournament?" Spencer's voice echoed through the room.

I froze.

Coach Wilder sighed.

The jumbo basketball shoes halted in mid thud.

Spencer turned around in his seat in the front row. He stared at me, eyes wide. "You think we're good enough? You have that much confidence in us?" He shook his head in wonder. "Wow."

"I—uh—"

I swallowed. I glanced up at Coach Wilder, hoping for rescue, hoping for more first aid facts.

He gazed back. Cocked an eyebrow at me.

"Yes," I said. "I think we could be good enough."

The room giggled. Somewhere behind me, Wesley snorted.

I let out a Breath of Doom and leaned over to dig the neatly folded sheet of paper from my shoe.

I hadn't planned on breaking it out right here in the middle of health class, with Coach Wilder and the Kaleys and Wesley Banks, of all people, and even Sam watching me. But if I couldn't have a speech bubble bobbing over my head, I could have the next best thing: an actual speech. I couldn't guarantee my voice wouldn't go all wonky while I read it, but it would still be better than having my words jam in my throat so nothing came out at all.

I unfolded the speech bubble. I held it in both hands. "I've written down the reasons."

Wesley laughed. "This I got to hear."

I swallowed. And started reading.

Here in Art Club, we are happy, confident, smart people. Except Earhart Middle doesn't know it. We tried to show them at the assembly, but as we sadly remember, nobody saw our big finish.

But now we have a chance for an even bigger finish. A finish everyone will see. A finish that will keep us from being vaporized into the Wasteland of Unwanted Clubs, along with Comic Book Collectors and the Square Dance Team.

I glanced over the top of my speech bubble and accidentally caught Sam's eye. I braced myself for one of her fatal glares. But she actually looked . . . proud?

I guess because I'd used her startling yearbook discovery.

Noah was doing his best to look encouraging.

And Spencer was nodding.

But the rest of Art Club just watched me. Eyes narrow. Chins set. Arms crossed over their chests.

I took a breath and plunged ahead.

A finish that will get our bulletin board back for good. Because how could Mr. Petrucelli keep a bulletin board from the winners of the biggest event of the entire school year?

That's right. I'm talking about Last Player Standing. Before you throw paintbrushes at me, think about this:

1. Art Club works great as a team. We proved that during our assembly.
2. Since we're smart, we can figure out strategy.
3. Since we're not athletic, we won't be a bunch of hot dogs and ball hogs. That has to be a plus. Right?

Out of the corner of my eye, I saw Coach Wilder nod.

That was my big finish. That was where Art Club

4. We'd have the best team name in the whole tournament: the Artful Dodgers.
5. If we win—no, <u>when we win</u>—we'll never have to worry about anyone taking anything away from us again. Not our bulletin board. Not our assembly.

Not anything.

was supposed to cheer and lift me onto their shoulders and carry me down the hall to the school office, where we could turn in our completely filled-out dodgeball roster.

But when the last words came stumbling out into the dead silence, they sounded completely lame, even to me.

"Okay, look." I closed my eyes. "This"—I waved the speech bubble—"is all true. The part about us being smart? That's true. And the part about working together? That's true, too. And having the best team name? Completely true." I let out a breath. Finally worked up the courage to look Art Club in the eye. "But that's not why I signed us up."

Art Club watched me.

"I know you thought I was doing all this for Art Club," I said. "Like I was some kind of Art Club superhero, trying to save the bulletin board and keep us in the yearbook and everything. And I wanted to do all that stuff. I did. But mainly I did it for myself. So I could get the helmet."

The silence grew heavier.

"The helmet?" Spencer looked at me, his face squinched into a confused frown. "The *batting* helmet? But . . . you don't play baseball."

Wesley snorted. "That's what I told his little dork of a brother."

"He's not a dork." I clenched my fists. Clenched my speech bubble into a tight ball. "He's a little kid." I looked at Art Club. "He's a little kid who wanted that batting helmet more than he ever wanted anything in the entire world, and because of me, he didn't get it. Wesley did. So yeah, I tried to drag all of you into the last thing you'd ever sign up to do because I wanted to make it up to him. I'm sorry."

I closed my eyes. It sounded even more despicable when I said it out loud like that.

"So . . . you did all this for your brother?" said Spencer. "The comic book pages and now this." He waved a hand toward the crumpled speech bubble. "The dodgeball team?"

I nodded.

177

Spencer shot Martin Higby a sideways glance, and Martin shot his own sideways glance at Gretchen Klamm, who shot a glance at Olivia and her black smudges.

Nobody said anything for a very long moment.

Then Spencer gave a sharp nod. "If I'm Last Player Standing," he said, "I'll give the helmet to your brother."

I looked at him, confused.

"Me too," said Martin.

"And me," said Gretchen. "Like that'll ever happen. But if it does, the helmet definitely goes to your brother."

Spencer rose from his seat, pulled a ballpoint pen from his pocket with a big flourish, and strode across the room. He stopped beside my desk, pulled the pink roster out from under my health notebook, clicked his pen . . . and printed his name across the top line.

He crossed the second t in "Osterholtz" with a crisp straight line, then turned and handed his pen to Martin.

Martin signed under Spencer.

Then Gretchen.

Then Olivia, who signed in charcoal.

And then everybody else in Art Club, including Dillon after Sam glared him into it.

I couldn't believe it. They'd all signed up. Every single one of them. And I didn't have to fast-talk them into it. All I had to do was tell the truth. They did it for Beech.

But that still only made ten of us. I pulled the roster toward me. We still had four blank spaces—two players and two alternates.

Noah picked up the pen and spun the roster around to face him. "I can be an alternate." He gave me a serious look. "I'm counting on you to never put me in the game."

"Not a problem." I stopped. "But I thought the band had a team."

"They do." He shrugged. "But the band is pretty big and, thankfully, the woodwind section didn't make the cut. Brass and percussion are a lot more aggressive. The drum line can bob and weave like nobody's business, and our tuba player's a maniac. She has amazing arm strength. So I'm available to ride your bench."

He printed his name on the first alternate line.

"Give me that." Sam had stomped up behind him, and now she snatched the pen from his hand. She mowed me down with a Zawicki Glare of Don't-Even-*Think*-I'm-Doing-Something-Nice-for-You-'Cause-I'm-Not. "I have to be there anyway to keep an eye on Dillon. I might as well sit close."

She printed her name under Noah's.

So we had our alternates.

Coach Wilder gave a thoughtful nod. "Two short."

I nodded too.

He swept a quick gaze around the room and stopped on a slope-shouldered kid in the back row.

"Skeet," he said.

Owen froze. He gave Coach Wilder a terrified look from under his hair.

"You're on the basketball team."

Owen gave a terrified nod.

"Are you playing dodgeball for them?"

Owen looked at Coach, then at Wesley. He gave an embarrassed shake of his head. "No."

Wesley shrugged. "We're in it to win it. Had to cut the deadwood. Nothing personal."

Owen narrowed his eyes. He gave Wesley a glare. A glare that looked like it had been burning for a long while.

And it occurred to me for the first time that maybe not everybody believed Wesley was the superhero of Earhart Middle. Maybe other people had noticed that he didn't use his powers for good. Maybe they knew he was a supervillain in disguise.

Owen rose to his feet, straightened his shoulders from their usual hunch, and gave a jerk of his head to his friend Curtis, who was sitting next to him. Curtis warmed the bench on the basketball team too but was built more like a fireplug, and as Owen loped toward my desk, Curtis followed after him in a nervous, fireplug trot.

Owen looked at Wesley. Looked him square in the eye. "Maybe *that* wasn't personal," he said. "But this is."

He picked up the pen. Signed his name without taking his eyes off Wesley. He handed the pen to Curtis, who nervously signed, then skittered back to his desk.

"So you got yourself a little team." Wesley turned and swaggered out of the room. "Good luck with that, *Tut*." The door banged shut behind him.

Spencer picked up the roster. "Wow," he said. "Wesley's right. We *do* have a team. All the lines are filled in. All we need now is the sponsor signature." He looked up at me, panic in his eyes. "And Mrs. Frazee has the flu."

"Not a problem." Coach Wilder gave the ballpoint pen a click.

Sponsor Signature: *Coach Wilder*

"Mrs. Frazee can be cosponsor once she gets back." He looked up at me. "MacBean. Turn this in at

181

the office." He handed me the roster. "Then run down and take the sign off the art room door."

"Yes, sir," I said.

He clicked the pen again. "Art Club is no longer canceled."

Tucker MacBean's Top Secret Undercover
Beanboy Comic Book Page #6:

thirty

I've always believed that every person is born with some kind of talent. Like I was a born comic book artist. And Noah was born with all those giant brain cells. And even somebody like the Kaleys, they were born knowing how to boss people around. Which took talent, and probably a lot of stamina, seeing as how they kept at it nonstop without ever stepping off the gas.

But whatever talent Dillon Zawicki was born with, he did a good job of keeping it secret.

"So. Hey," I said to him that afternoon when I ambled into the art room.

Dillon didn't say anything. He'd pretty much commandeered my desk. (And I pretty much let him. I mean, when a water buffalo lays claim to your desk, what can a field mouse do?) Now he lounged on the tilty desktop.

"So." I tried again. "Thanks for joining up. Even if Sam made you. You really filled out our roster."

Nothing.

Coach Wilder strode into the room, Noah on his heels. Noah carried my clipboard tucked sharply under his arm.

"Let's get to it," said Coach Wilder. "We've got a lot to learn, and only two weeks to learn it."

He lined us up in a long row.

Well, not all of us.

Dillon stayed where he was.

Coach Wilder paced in front of us, a drill sergeant inspecting his troops.

Noah stood off to the side, clipboard at the ready, a faithful second in command.

Dillon propped his head on his hand so he could watch, and then I guess after a while that took too much effort, so he just stretched out and flopped his head on his arm. Didn't talk. Didn't move. Didn't drool, either, so I guess he wasn't asleep.

Coach Wilder stopped in front of us, feet planted wide, arms crossed over his sweatshirt.

"Show of hands," said Coach Wilder. "How many of you have played dodgeball before?"

Owen's hand shot straight up, with Curtis's right behind.

The rest of us stole sideways frowns at each other. On the face of it, Coach Wilder's question seemed fairly straightforward, but the answer was a little tricky.

Spencer sneaked a timid hand into the air.

Coach Wilder gave him a sharp nod. "You've played dodgeball, son?"

"That depends." Spencer slid his hand back down. "When you say 'played,' do you mean voluntarily? Or are you also counting forced dodgeball games against our will in PE? And again, that term 'played.' Does it refer to active participation? Or cowering at the back of the gym till a ball finally hits you so you can go sit down—does that count too?"

Coach Wilder's face wrinkled into a frown. "Forced against your—what? I don't—okay, never mind." He rubbed his temple. "We'll just say we're starting at zero."

Which, for us, was probably the best place to start.

We pushed all the desks to the side of the room. (Except mine. It was already in the corner, with Dillon sprawled all over it.)

Coach Wilder rolled in a big canvas cart on wheels, filled with different-colored balls. He plucked one out. It looked like a red rubber grapefruit.

"This"—he squished the ball in his beefy fingers—"is a dodgeball."

With a snap of his arm, he whipped it at Spencer. Whipped it right at him and hit him smack in the gut.

Spencer hunched over. Clutched his stomach. I could tell he was gearing up to yowl in pain.

But instead, he blinked.

"Hey!" Spencer straightened up. "That didn't even hurt."

He hiked his jeans up and scrambled to retrieve the ball from under Mrs. Frazee's desk. He handed it back to Coach Wilder.

"No. It didn't hurt," said Coach. "It's foam. Slick on the outside. Soft on the inside. You don't want to get hit because that's the whole point of the game: dodge the ball. But you don't have to be scared. The ball's not going to hurt you."

He dropped the ball back into the cart.

"Now then, you've all seen this dodgeball tournament before," he said. "What usually happens?"

Owen raised his hand again, happy to suddenly be the expert at something, I guess. "Every man for himself, Coach. Pick up the balls. Slam them into the other team. Everybody trying to be Last Player Standing."

"Right." Coach nodded. "We're not going to fall into that trap. You can't win all by yourself. You got to work as a team. We're going to go through some drills, see what everybody's good at, and set up our team strategy so that each player will do what he or she does best."

Spencer's eyes grew wide. "You may not know this, Coach, but that's the exact strategy Art Club is completely excellent at. Tucker does comic books because that's his best thing. Gretchen weaves artistic belts because she's not good at comic books. Martin draws race cars because, well, we don't know why. But we're totally onboard with the do-what-you're-good-at strategy. That's something that will completely work for us. Wow." He shook his head. "One practice and already you get us. You're going to be a great coach. Wait till Mrs. Frazee gets back. Then we'll have *two* great coaches."

Coach raised an eyebrow. "Thanks. I think. Okay, let's get started."

He rolled the ball cart to the other end of the room, then used a roll of athletic tape to make a circle near the bottom of the supply-cabinet door.

He ambled back to the cart. "That's what you're aiming for. Their feet. You know why?"

"Can't catch it," said Owen, our resident dodgeball authority.

Coach nodded. "That's right. They can't catch it."

He snatched one of the balls from the cart and whipped it at me. Whipped it at my ankles.

I did a little dance, jerking up one foot, then the

other. Too little too late. *Smack.* The ball slammed into my ankle.

"See?" Coach nodded. "Tucker couldn't catch it. But what if I did this?"

Coach snatched up another ball. Tossed it into the air above Martin's head. An easy toss. A total bunny.

Martin held out his hands, weaving this way and that under the ball.

"I'm not sure I can catch *that,* either, Coach," he said.

The ball dropped through Martin's hands and bounced off his foot.

Coach Wilder closed his eyes. Pinched the bridge of his nose. "We've got some work to do."

We lined up by the cart and took turns throwing at the taped circle.

Spencer couldn't even hit the supply closet. Forget about the door. Or the circle. Martin's ball bounced twice on the floor and rolled to a stop before it *got* to the door. Gretchen could hit the circle, but only with a really soft underhand throw, which was just asking to be caught. Owen did pretty well. He threw hard. But way off the mark.

Then I stepped up to the ball cart. My first throw curved in the air like a rainbow. Landed with a light thud in front of the door. My second ball hooked wide left. It would've taken Noah's clipboard right out of his hands if it'd had any velocity behind it. My third throw was hard. Bounced about three feet in front of me and wanged off under a drying rack.

"Dude. That's messed up."

The voice echoed through the room. At first we couldn't figure out where it came from.

Then we remembered Dillon.

"Doesn't anybody in this place know how to throw?"

He let out a major breath, scraped my tall art stool back, and heaved himself from my desk. He plodded toward the cart.

"This is how you throw," he said.

He snatched up a ball and hurled it toward the supply closet.

BAM.

It slammed into the door, smack in the middle of the circle.

Before we could blink, he'd snatched up another ball.

BAM.

Then another.

BAM.

We stared at him.

It was as if we'd wakened a sleeping giant.

He snatched up a handful of balls in his left hand and transferred them, one after another, to his right, his throwing hand.

BAM.

BAM.

BAM.

BAM.

The balls slammed into Coach Wilder's circle. Art Club stood there watching, jaws hanging open.

Yeah. Dillon Zawicki was born with a talent.

thirty-one

After one practice, we all knew what we were good at.

And we were good at a lot more than I expected.

I unzipped my coat and followed Beech as he wound his way through tables and waitresses across the Atomic Flapjack.

Art Club had Dillon, of course, whose throws were so hard and so accurate, he could've drilled a hole right through the supply-closet door if the balls had been anything but foam. And Gretchen, who seemed to have ball magnets in her arms. She could catch anything, which made sense—all that belt weaving had given her amazing hand-eye coordination. And Spencer, who was a big surprise. He darted this way and that around the art room, all quick and disjointed. Nobody could hit him because nobody knew where he'd dart next.

Those were some pretty good skills. Still, I wasn't sure they were enough to win a tournament. Especially against Wesley and the Sundances.

I unzipped Beech. He wrestled out of his coat and squeaked on his knees across the slick red vinyl of the booth seat. It was the big round booth in the corner—our regular Laundry Day booth—and Beech knee-scooted to his usual spot in the exact center of the round part. I pulled my coat off and slid in on the end. My stomach grumbled.

The Atomic Flapjack was pretty crowded, and the clink of silverware and murmur of conversation filled the air. The smell of freshly sizzled bacon and hot pancakes whirled around us.

Almost made me dizzy, I was so hungry.

"Hey, guys." Our regular Laundry Day waitress—Phyllis—slid three Atomic Flapjack place mats and two glasses of orange juice onto the table. One for me and one for Beech. "You already got your laundry in?"

I nodded. "Mom's feeding the machines."

On Laundry Day, Beecher and I helped Mom haul the laundry baskets from the car into the laundromat. (Beech carried the dryer sheets.) We sorted the laundry and threw it into the washers (Beech was in charge of standing beside the jug of detergent), and then Mom sent us ahead to the Flapjack while she added soap, slipped in the quarters, and got the machines chugging along, sudsing up our dirty clothes. She always caught up to us at almost the exact time Phyllis slid our breakfast onto the table. We had our timing down perfect.

Phylllis placed a coffee cup and a big silver pot of coffee next to Mom's place, then reached in her pocket and pulled out an Atomic Flapjack coloring page and a handful of crayons. She set them in front of Beech.

"Have fun," she said. "Your food shouldn't take long."

She turned on her sensible white waitress shoes and strode off. She didn't leave menus for us. She didn't have to. She knew our regular Laundry Day breakfast order by heart: teddy bear pancake with a chocolate chip face for Beech, French toast for me, veggie omelet for Mom.

I reached over for one of Beecher's crayons. Not the red one. That was his favorite, and I didn't want to hear him scream. I picked up the green.

"Can I borrow this for a minute?"

Beech looked up from his coloring page, studied the crayon in my hand, and nodded.

I slid my paper Atomic Flapjack place mat toward me and started writing.

STRATEGY

1. Throwing - Dillon
2. Catching - Gretchen
3. Dodging
4. Teamwork

Beech leaned over to study my scribbles.

"What doing?" he said.

"Trying to figure out dodgeball strategy." I shook my head. "Who would have figured Dillon Zawicki as a human cannon? That kid can flat out throw. And nobody even knew."

I was mostly talking to myself, saying it out loud, trying to get it sorted in my brain.

But Beech nodded. With authority. "I know," he said.

I looked at him. "You know what?"

"Dillon throw. Throw shoe. Throw shirt." He counted on his fingers. "Throw paper. Throw underwear."

"He threw underwear?"

Beech shrugged. "Sam say."

Yeah. I'm sure she did. I could almost hear her growly voice inside my head now: *"Well yeah, he can throw. How do you think he got the sneakers up on the gym lights?"*

Dillon's born talent was right there, in front of my face, the whole time. It made perfect sense, and until this very minute I hadn't figured it out.

Beech went back to his Flapjack page. I watched him color for a minute. He pressed really hard and colored everything red. The stars, the planets, the pancake spaceships. By the time Phyllis got that red crayon back, it wouldn't be more than a nub. A nub with all the paper peeled off.

"Beech," I said, "I know you're mad at me for not being a superhero—"

"You superhero," he said, without looking up.

I blinked. "I am?"

"You win," he said, still coloring. "Win big."

"But I thought you were mad at me. About, you know, the Iron Man helmet. I wasn't a superhero anymore because I couldn't get it back for you."

"You superhero," he muttered into his coloring page. "I not superhero."

I gave him a confused frown. "What do you mean you're not a superhero?"

He looked up finally. He blew out a breath. "No helmet," he said. "No helmet. No Ine Man. No superhero. No. Superhero. *Know* that?" He looked at me hard, like he was trying to drill the information into my brain with his eyes.

"Okay," I said. "Calm down. I know that."

I took a sip of my orange juice and thought about this. Beech wasn't upset because I wasn't a superhero anymore. He was upset because *he* wasn't a superhero. I'd been making everything about me, and this wasn't about me at all.

"You're kind of a superhero," I told him.

He looked up again, eyes narrowed.

"I mean, stuff's harder for you," I said, "but you do it anyway. That's what superheroes do."

He considered this for a minute. Then went back to coloring.

"Not save people," he said.

Well, that was true. But he still thought I was a superhero, and I never saved anybody either.

"What if you had the helmet?" I said.

"I not." He kept coloring.

"I know. But what if you did?"

He looked up again.

"I not," he said. "*He* have helmet. He not super-hero."

Beecher set down his red crayon and let out a heavy sigh.

"Everything nice." He spread his hands wide, showing how big and nice everything was. "Then he? Mean." He pushed his hands together in a little point, showing Wesley's little wedge of mean.

He was right. Wesley Banks *wasn't* a superhero, no matter how many helmets he bought, because he didn't use his powers for nice. He used them for mean. Even my goober of a little brother—a kid who couldn't eat his food unless it had a face, a kid who had to go up and down stairs sitting on his butt— even he had figured *that* one out.

Why couldn't Earhart Middle?

I looked at his hands. At Beecher's hands pressed into a wedge. When Wesley was using his super-powers for mean, he was exactly like that. He zeroed in like a laser, like the sharp little point Beecher had made with his hands.

I thought about that day in the lunchroom. Wesley had been so busy tripping me with his giant feet, he didn't even notice that somebody at his own table grabbed me before I fell on my face. And then in Coach Wilder's room. Wesley was so zoned in to humiliating me with my roster, he didn't see when Owen Skeet, a player on his very own basketball team, a guy who, along with all the other basketball players, had followed him through the halls of Earhart Middle like a puppy trotting after his master, who sat at the table next to Wesley's at lunch just so he could maybe soak up some of his reflected cool, that kid, in a single instant, stood up and quit being Wesley's puppy. He convinced Curtis to quit being a puppy too.

And Wesley didn't notice.

I tapped my crayon against the place mat and thought about this.

A blast of cold air whipped through the Flapjack. I glanced up, thinking maybe Mom was already here.

But it wasn't Mom. It was some other family. I went back to my place-mat list.

"Hey!" Beech climbed onto his knees on the booth seat. "Mrs. Hottins!"

Before I could figure out what he was talking about, he scrambled across the slick vinyl, climbed down the other side, and shot across the Atomic Flapjack, weaving around tables and chairs and under the arms of a waitress carrying plates of hot breakfast.

"Great." I dropped the crayon and wove my way through the restaurant after him.

This new family was standing inside the doorway, shaking off the cold. Beecher plunged right into them. Plunged into the mom.

"Mrs. *Hottins.*" He fell against her and hugged her

legs, eyes closed, cheek pressed against her winter coat. "You *here*," he said.

I'd never met his teacher before, but I figured this must be her. Otherwise Beech was attacking a complete stranger.

"Hey there, Beecher." Mrs. Hottins patted his shoulder. "What a nice surprise. I didn't expect to see you here."

"We always here," Beech told her legs. "Now you here too."

Mrs. Hottins ran a hand over his head, then leaned down and peeled him away. "What do we talk about in school? We talk about how hugs aren't appropriate outside your family, right? How, when you meet your friends, it's better to fist bump or shake hands. Right?"

"Right." Beech held up his fist and bumped her. Then he collapsed against her again.

"Sorry." I reached down and dragged Beech off poor Mrs. Hottins. I wrapped my arm around his chest so he wouldn't glue himself back onto her legs again.

Mrs. Hottins laughed. "Don't worry about it. We do this all the time. I imagine we'll have this same conversation Monday when you get to school, won't we, Beecher?"

By this time Phyllis had arrived, menus tucked under her arm. "Table for four?" she asked Mrs. Hottins.

"Your teacher has to go sit down now, Beech," I told him. "Tell her you'll see her later."

"See you later," said Beech.

I tried to angle him toward our booth. And as I turned, I noticed the rest of her family. Her husband, I guess. And her sons. One younger and one about my age.

No, *exactly* my age.

I stopped, dead frozen, right there in the middle of the Atomic Flapjack.

Because Beecher's teacher wasn't Mrs. Hottins. She was Mrs. Hawkins.

And she wasn't just Beecher's teacher.

She was the mother of one of the Sundances.

The mother of T.J.

T.J. Hawkins.

Who had been milling around behind his dad this whole time, scrutinizing the specials scrawled on the chalkboard by the door.

Now he cut his glance from the specials—

—and accidentally looked right at me.

His eyes grew wide and his cheeks turned pink. He whipped his head away again to give the chalkboard more scrutiny.

Who could blame him? I was completely staring at him. I'm sure my mouth was hanging open, I was staring that hard.

But after studying the chalkboard for a minute,

he flicked his eyes back. He met my eyes. And raised his chin at me, in a half nod.

I was surprised at first. Then I half nodded back.

Then T.J. noticed Beech standing there holding up his clenched fist.

T.J. looked startled for a second, like he wasn't sure what he was supposed to do. But then he held up his fist. Gave Beech a tap. He quickly turned and followed his mom and their waitress across the Atomic Flapjack.

Tucker MacBean's Top Secret Undercover Beanboy Comic Book Page #7:

thirty-two

"It's up!"

Spencer's voice rose above the roar of Earhart middle-schoolers swarming down the hall toward the cafeteria. Spencer leaped above them like a Ping-Pong ball, his arm stretched in the air so we could locate him.

Noah and I followed Spencer's upraised hand to a mob of kids knotted around the window of the middle school office. And for maybe the first time in his life, Spencer's rubber-band body and pointy elbows were paying off. He had wormed his way between fellow students till he'd reached the office window.

"Checkmates!" he hollered back to us. "First round we got the Checkmates."

Noah and I slapped each other a high-five. I'd

read Noah's scouting report. The Checkmates tackled dodgeball like they tackled chess. They were excellent at strategy, but by the time they studied the court, ran through each option in their heads, and settled on their next move, they'd all been pummeled with balls and were sitting in the jail. Game over.

Noah and I pushed forward and finally reached the office window, where Mr. Petrucelli had taped the tournament bracket on the inside, facing out, so the mob could breathe all over the glass without mangling the paper bracket.

I traced my finger across the bracket.

★ LAST PLAYER STANDING ★

Backcourt Bombers
Nuclear Reactors
Total Takedown
Beethoven's Blitz
Basketball Blast
Calculators
Checkmates
Artful Dodgers

Winner

Round I   Semifinals   Final

"If we beat the Checkmates—"

"When," said Noah.

"Right. *When* we beat the Checkmates, we'll face off against either girls' basketball or the math team in the second round."

I ran my finger up the bracket till I got to another team: the Backcourt Bombers.

"I imagine the Bombers will win their first two games," I said.

Here's where I was hoping Noah would consult the scouting report in his head and give me a reason the Backcourt Bombers would completely lose in the opening round.

Instead he nodded.

"Which means we'll face Wesley in the championship," I said.

Noah nodded again.

"We'll just have to make sure we get that far," I said.

Tucker MacBean's Top Secret Undercover
Beanboy Comic Book Page #8:

thirty-three

You may be wondering why I kept drawing comic book pages. After all, we'd filled our roster and had officially become a dodgeball team.

I had two very good reasons.

No, three.

Actually, four:

1. Even though we were completely going to win the tournament and snag the helmet for Beech, there was still a possibility that, well, we wouldn't. And then there we'd be, all fourteen of us, with no bulletin board. We'd still need more members.

2. Earhart Middle had gotten hooked on Beanboy. On days when no page showed up,

they were bummed. My finely tuned hearing picked up comments like "Don't tell me they've stopped. I want to see the end of the story." So I had to keep drawing. A comic book artist never wants to disappoint his fans.

3. The Phantom Photocopier. I wasn't sure who it was. It might still be Mrs. Frazee, dragging herself from her sick bed, copying my pages in her fevered state. But whoever it was, she was counting on me. After everything the Phantom had done, I couldn't let her down.

4. Emma thought it was cool.

I wandered into the art room, wondering what Coach Wilder had planned for practice today—

—and nearly got flattened by Spencer.

"Tucker! Hey, Tuck!" He bounded up to me like a new puppy, his knitted hat flopping, his tail practically wagging. For one horrifying second I thought he might lick me.

"My great-aunt finished it last night," he said. "What do you think?"

He did a little turn so I could get the full impact: his new hand-knitted vest. Red and white (our school colors), with brushes, pencils, and paint tubes worked into the pattern. His last name—OSTERHOLTZ—was embroidered across the back, like on a team jersey.

"It's the Official Artful Dodger Dodgeball Uniform," he said. "Great-Aunt Bernice is ready to get started on the rest, so before we begin practicing, I need to write down everyone's size." He held a sheet of paper and a pencil at the ready.

I stared at him. "That's—I don't even—wow."

That's what my mouth said out loud.

Here's what my head said inside: *No. Way. No way in this universe will I put anything like that on my body. I don't care what you do—pull out my toenails, throw me in a tank of alligators, let Sam Zawicki yell in my face for the rest of my life—it's never going to happen.*

"No way." The words rasped through the art room. "Not happening."

My eyes popped wide. I clapped my hand over my mouth. Had it lost all control again? Had my mouth said those words out loud?

Spencer's eyes popped wide too. He clenched the paper in two white-knuckled fists and turned to peer into the depths of the art room.

Dillon Zawicki was perched once more at my desk, his meaty head propped up with one meaty palm.

"I don't wear vests," he said, "and I'm sure not wearing some loser vest with little pictures on it."

Now the paper started shaking, Spencer was

210

gripping it so tight. I was afraid it might snap in two. Heck, I was afraid *Spencer* might snap in two. His whole body quivered, fired up to do ... something. Defend his honor. Defend his great-aunt's honor. Defend the honor of knitted vests everywhere. He was all puffed up, like an enraged baby chicken who *forgot* he was a baby chicken.

"If you're dead set on knitted stuff, do a hat." Dillon squinted at Spencer. "Like what you're wearing, only not puffy. Snug, you know? And none of this red and white stuff with fluffy little balls. Plain black. And snug. I'd wear that."

Tucker MacBean's
← 7th grade
school picture

instant bump
in coolness
factor →

I blinked. I'd wear that too.

Spencer was still staring at Dillon, eyes narrowed, mouth pressed into such a hard knot of rage that his lips had disappeared.

"You know," I told him, in my most soothing voice, "Dillon may have a point. Now wait." I held up a hand. "Hear me out. As amazing as your vest is, and wow, it's just—I can't even—wow. But that kind of amazement takes time, and we've only got a week till the tournament. Your great-aunt would knit her fingers right off trying to make that kind of deadline. We can't do that to her, Spencer. We just can't."

Spencer nodded. "I never thought of it that way. Fourteen vests *are* an awful big undertaking." He chewed his lip. "But she could whip out three, four hats per day."

"Well, there you go," I said. "Plus she wouldn't have to worry about sizes. They could all be the same. Except for, well"—I cut my eyes covertly toward Dillon—"maybe one extra large."

Spencer thought about this for a moment. Then he leaned toward me. "He doesn't *deserve* a nice hat," he whispered, "but it would look funny if he was the only one not wearing one, so I think I should be the bigger person." He made a couple of scribbles on his sheet of paper, then looked up. "Would it be okay if I went ahead and wore my vest anyway? It would make my great-aunt really proud and it wouldn't encumber my throwing arm in any way."

"That would be great," I said. "That would be one hundred percent great."

Coach trundled the ball cart through the door. He tossed a roll of athletic tape at Dillon, who snagged it out of the air with one meaty paw.

"We need lines on the floor," Coach told him.

Dillon heaved himself from his seat and started taping gym lines across the gritty concrete. Coach wheeled the cart to the center of the room. The rest of Art Club began pushing desks against the wall.

"Oh . . . *my*."

We looked up—

—and froze. Even Coach Wilder.

Mrs. Frazee stood in the doorway. Her nose was red, her eyes runny, and she clasped a Kleenex tight to her mouth. She sniffed, and the hand-dyed scarf about her neck trembled.

I looked at Spencer. His eyes were wide with horror.

We'd made her cry. We'd taken over Mrs. Frazee's room, turned it into a dodgeball court, shoved all the art equipment against the wall.

And made her cry.

Mrs. Frazee clapped her hands together. "Performance art!" She tossed her Kleenex into the air like confetti. "I abandoned you, stuck at home with this tedious flu, but you found a way to push your performance art in a new direction that speaks perfectly to your middle school experience."

Which Coach Wilder didn't get.

But Art Club actually did.

Because when we thought about combining different media—in this case dodgeballs and gym shoes—to convey our idea, it made sense to us.

A lot more sense than trying to convince ourselves we were athletic suddenly.

"And our knitted caps fit right in," Spencer whispered to me. "They're the art part of the performance art. Wait till I tell Great-Aunt Bernice."

Dillon ripped the last piece of tape off with his teeth, Coach Wilder lined up the balls, and Mrs. Frazee helped organize us into what she called our "parts"—which was basically the dodgeball skills we were each best at.

While Art Club warmed up, I sidled over to Mrs. Frazee.

"So," I said casually. "You must do a lot of photocopying, huh? I mean, in your capacity as an art teacher."

Mrs. Frazee shook her head. Her big turquoise earrings jangled.

"Not really," she said. "Permission slips sometimes. And once in a while a supply list. But I stay away from copiers, computers, any kind of electronic gadgets, as much as I can. I like a more personal touch."

That was true. Last semester when she sent home progress reports, they were hand-lettered and folded into origami zoo animals.

But if Mrs. Frazee wasn't the Phantom Photocopier, who was?

Coach Wilder ran us through the drills. Footwork. Arm work. Dodging. Scooping. Catching. Aiming. Throwing. Mrs. Frazee directed what she called Themes and Communications Between Performers (a.k.a. dodgeball players).

And Mrs. Frazee was right. When we thought about it like performance art—about each of us playing our part—we were good. Really good.

We worked together, throwing, catching, scooping up balls, hollering out plays.

When practice was over and we were all standing there, pink-cheeked, out of breath, hunched over with our hands on our knees, we couldn't help smiling. And slapping high-fives.

"Good practice," said Coach Wilder. "A lot better than I expected."

We gathered up the balls, and as Coach wheeled the cart past Mrs. Frazee, he shook his head.

"Performance art, huh?" he said to her. "Wonder if that would work in football."

thirty-four

I bounced on the balls of my feet to let off pent-up adrenaline. I glanced around the gym.

Mom and Beech were planted on the bleachers, front row, midcourt. Beech had put his pillowcase cape on again, and his arm was wrapped around a big bag of popcorn. He saw me looking at him and stopped munching long enough to wave.

"Go, Tut! Win!" He punched the air with his fist. His voice echoed through the cavernous gym.

Mom was chatting with Sam's grandpa, who sat forward in his seat, elbows on his knees, work-worn hands clasped together, watching Dillon warm up (which, for Dillon, meant giving his knuckles a loud crack). Pure pride sparkled in his old blue eyes.

He'd bought Dillon a new pair of tennis shoes for the tournament, and now Dillon stood there, fists on his hips, eyes narrowed and fierce as he studied our opponent—the Checkmates. His extra-large black knitted cap was pulled snug over his head. If it'd had horns jutting out the sides, he would've looked like a Viking.

A few other parents were scattered through the bleachers. But other than that, the gym was pretty much empty.

Which was weird.

The tournament was only one part of the school carnival. The rest of the school was filled with games and food and the silent auction.

But this was Last Player Standing, the biggest event of the carnival. The carnival? It was the biggest event of the school year.

And hardly anybody had shown up.

As I rolled my shoulders and tipped my head from side to side, stretching my neck, two kids from Earhart Middle wandered into the gym. They frowned at the empty bleachers.

The first kid shook his head. "I thought there was supposed to be a game."

"Me too." The other kid dug a bracket out of the pocket of his cargo pants. He studied it. "Eh. Chess geeks and art losers."

The first kid jerked his head toward the door. "C'mon. Let's see what kind of prizes we can score in the ring toss. We can come back when there's a real game."

Well. That explained it.

But that was okay. It would give the Artful Dodgers a chance to get our dodgeball legs under us without a big crowd breathing down our necks.

The referee lined up the balls on the centerline. The players took up positions. The ref blew her whistle, and we rocketed toward the line in the opening rush.

Noah's scouting report was dead on. The Checkmates had a game plan, and you could tell they'd put real thought into it. They had mentally divided their side of the court into squares and assigned each of their players a square. They also assigned each player on the opposing team (us) the name of a chess piece. Dillon was our king, of course. Spencer was a knight because he moved over the court all cattywampus. I think I was a pawn, which was not a real confidence booster. The Checkmates targeted each of our players according to how valuable he was to us. They figured if they could take our king—Dillon—the game would pretty much be over.

Which was solid strategy. It could've worked.

Except while they were busy lining themselves

219

up in squares, our king was busy mowing them down with dodgeballs. Before they could pick off even one of our pawns, their whole side was out.

The ref blew her whistle. "Game over!"

Art Club whooped and leaped together in a giant group chest bump.

Mrs. Frazee jangled.

Coach Wilder let out a low, growly "Yeah" and paced along the sideline, nodding his approval.

The crowd cheered. (Okay, Mom and Beech and Sam's grandpa cheered. Some of the other people clapped politely.)

Even Sam did a solid fist clench.

Noah made some kind of notation on his clipboard, then caught my eye and raised one finger in the air.

One down.

Two to go.

And from this point on, it was only going to get harder.

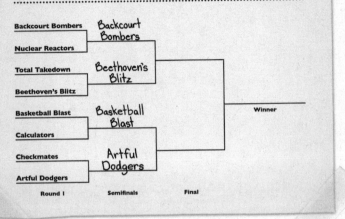

☆ LAST PLAYER STANDING ☆

	Round 1	Semifinals	Final	
Backcourt Bombers	Backcourt Bombers			
Nuclear Reactors		Beethoven's Blitz		
Total Takedown	Beethoven's Blitz			
Beethoven's Blitz			Winner	
Basketball Blast	Basketball Blast			
Calculators		Artful Dodgers		
Checkmates	Artful Dodgers			
Artful Dodgers				

221

thirty-five

"If you win, you can have your stupid bulletin board back."

Kaley T. crossed her arms over her chest. Kaley C. crossed her arms, too. They shot each other a look that clearly said, "Doesn't matter what we bet. These loser dweebs are *never* getting their bulletin board back." They smiled when they did it.

We were standing on the sidelines in front of the Artful Dodgers' jail. The game was about to start, and the gym had filled up considerably. Most of the crowd was sitting on the Basketball Blast side, gearing up to cheer on the girls' basketball team. The Artful Dodgers still had a smattering of diehard fans on our side, though: Mom, Beech, Sam's grandpa, some lady knitting what looked like a really long scarf (she had to be Great-Aunt Bernice), and the other Artful Dodgers' parents. The smell of popcorn wafted in from the carnival. Voices rumbled, feet clanked against the metal bleachers, and the louder the noise grew, the more sure I was that my heart would pound a dent right into my rib cage.

And now here were the Kaleys, standing side by side in their screaming pink tie-dyed Basketball Blast T-shirts and knee-high socks, arms crossed, eyes narrowed, staring us down as they tried to make a bet on our bulletin board.

"So?" said Kaley T. "Do we have a deal?"

The Artful Dodgers shot one another looks. Confused looks. Suspicious looks. Was this a joke? Some kind of mind trick to throw us off our game?

"What do you get if *you* win?" I said.

"You mean *when* we win?" Kaley T. rolled her eyes at Kaley C. "We get the bulletin board forever, no matter how much you whine to Mr. Petrucelli, no matter how many people you talk into signing up for your pathetic little club. Even if you get half the school—"

"The loser half," muttered Kaley C.

"—it won't matter. We keep the bulletin board."

Art Club was even more suspicious now.

But before we could figure out what to say, a low rasp split the air: "We'll take that bet."

I turned. Dillon towered over me. Over all of us.

He shrugged one massive shoulder. "Pink team's

just worried," he said. "Art Club already signed up a bunch of new members. If these guys would get to work"—he raised an eyebrow at Owen and Curtis, who tried to slink behind Gretchen—"they could drag in a few more of their basketball buddies, and *bam*, the bulletin board would be ours. Pink team's trying to stop that from happening. They're desperate."

Dillon Zawicki had taken one look at the Kaleys and figured out exactly what they were up to. There was a real brain ticking inside his T. *rex* body.

"Desperate?" Kaley T. nearly shrieked. "Ugh!"

She and Kaley C. turned on their sneakers (with matching pink laces) and stalked back to their side of the gym, muttering as they went.

"See? You try to help somebody and this is what you get," muttered Kaley T.

"I don't even know why these art losers signed up. They don't belong here," muttered Kaley C.

"No kidding. Don't they know this is a sport? We're going to slaughter them."

And then they giggled.

Dillon turned to me. "Don't worry. We got this."

He slapped me a high-five. About slapped my arm off.

The ref gave the signal and the players trotted onto the court—the Basketball Blast in matching pink vs. the Artful Dodgers with our cool black hats pulled snugly onto our heads (and one completely uncool red vest dangling from Spencer's scrawny shoulders).

We lined up. The crowd hushed. The ref blew her whistle and the opening rush was on.

The Blast weren't as organized as the Checkmates had been. But they were a lot faster, a lot stronger, and a heck of a lot more bloodthirsty. And anybody who ever laughed at someone for throwing like a girl clearly never saw a girl throw.

They whipped to the line, scooped back the balls, and started firing. And just that fast, Martin and Olivia went down, victims of ankle shots. They trudged over to sit in our jail.

The Blast kept firing. Balls pummeled us from every direction.

I have to be honest. The Artful Dodgers were stunned. It took us a few minutes to find our dodge-ball legs, and by that time we were down six players. Half our team.

But Owen was right. He said most dodgeball games were every player for himself—or herself. Chasing down balls. Slamming them into the other team. Nobody passing. Nobody working together. Everybody trying to be the rock star.

That's exactly what the Blast was doing.

And once we figured it out, once we got over the initial shock, once we got into our own rhythm, we started taking advantage of it.

Owen caught a ball in one arm, then a ball in the other, and just like that—*bang, bang*—two Blast players were out, and Martin and Gretchen were back in.

The Artful Dodgers kept dodging. Kept catching. Kept scooping up balls, passing to our best throwers, deflecting the other team's attention while our best throwers hammered them. We synchronized our efforts, stuck to our strategy, just like we practiced.

And the Blast kept doing what they did, which was that every single one of them gritted her teeth, played her own game, did everything she could to be Last Player Standing.

And one by one, they started going down.

We whittled away at their team till it was just the Kaleys and Emma against five of us.

Emma fired a ball at Owen's feet. It missed and bounced wide.

Spencer darted and dodged across the court, snatched up the ball, and whipped it backwards. Whipped it to me.

Emma had just thrown, was off balance, not looking at me. Making herself the perfect target.

I pulled the ball back. Steeled myself.

I hated throwing at Emma. I didn't want to be the one to take her down.

But just as I was taking aim, just as I was zeroing in on her ankles, another ball came whizzing from behind. About took my ear off. It whizzed past and—*smack*—hit Emma in the knee.

"Out!" called the ref.

I glanced over my shoulder.

Dillon gave me a quick chin lift. "Got your back, bro."

Emma dropped her ball and jogged toward her team's jail.

I felt bad for her because, well, she was Emma. But with her out, I could concentrate better on the game. Plus now we only had two players to target: Kaley T. and Kaley C.

Kaley C. seemed stunned. She lost focus for a second as she watched Emma leave the court.

And—*bam*—Dillon hammered her with a dodgeball.

And just like that, they were down to one. One player—Kaley T.—against five Artful Dodgers.

I clenched my fists. We had this. We could do it.

But Kaley T. was just as determined we couldn't.

"I am *not* letting a bunch of loser dweebs beat me," she growled.

She bared her teeth like a cornered tiger and started bombarding us.

Owen went down.

Then Gretchen.

Then me.

I trudged to our jail.

Only two Artful Dodgers left: Spencer and Dillon.

Which was okay. Great, in fact. If we could only have two players, those were the two I'd want: the kid who threw like a cannon and the kid who was impossible to hit.

Spencer did his thing: dodging and scooping. And Dillon did his: snatching up the balls Spencer scooped to him and firing them—BAM, BAM, BAM—at Kaley.

I have to give Kaley T. credit. She dodged. She weaved. She kept out of the line of fire for longer than I thought she would.

But then Dillon had her. He did. Kaley leaned over to snatch up a ball, and in that split second, he hurled his own dodgeball. Like a rocket, it shot across the gym.

Smack.

Slammed into her knee—

Yes!

—then popped up.

Popped straight up, almost in slow motion.

Kaley dropped her own ball and reached for it. Reached for it and gathered it in. Tripped and fell backwards, and I thought for sure the ball would bounce loose. But it didn't. She held on to it, clasped it against her chest as she went down. It was a catch. A fair catch. She'd caught Dillon's dodgeball.

"Out!" called the ref.

Dillon stood there, mouth open, before shaking his head and trudging toward our jail.

And now it was just Kaley T. . . . against Spencer. And his jumble of knees and elbows. And his hand-knitted vest.

And his total lack of throwing skill.

Spencer dodged and darted, bobbed and bounced. Kaley threw. And threw. And threw.

Missed every time, which wasn't a surprise to anyone. Spencer threw too. He had to. Each team had to throw at least every ten seconds, and Spencer was the only player our team had left.

Kaley was getting tired, I could tell. Tired of watching Spencer jump around. Tired of her throws completely missing. Tired of not winning the game already.

She hauled back and fired again.

Hard.

Too hard.

The throw was high.

Kaley T. knew it the minute she released the ball. She scrambled to fire off another one before Spencer could catch it.

Spencer hadn't caught another single ball during the whole tournament, but he didn't let that stop him.

"I goooooot iiiiiiit," he called as he careened about

the gym, vest flapping, trying to keep a bead on the ball.

Our jail rose to its toes, fists clenched, watching him.

The ball dropped. Thumped against his chest. And thumped right out again. Spencer scrambled. Pulled it back in. Tried to cradle it against his chest, but it got tangled in his knitted vest. One sneaker twisted under him and Spencer went down. Tumbled backwards, landed with a thud, butt first. The ball popped loose—

—and dropped into his lap.

Spencer clamped his arms down over it.

"Out!" called the ref. "Game over."

I whooped and threw my fist in the air. "Way to go, Spencer!"

"WHAT?" Kaley T. stormed toward the ref. "That's not fair! Did you see his stupid vest? *He* should be—"

I didn't hear the rest. The Artful Dodgers had erupted from our jail. Swarmed Spencer. Pulled him to his feet. Mrs. Frazee clapped and jangled. Coach Wilder allowed himself a low, tight fist pump and a sharp "Yeah!" as he paced along the sideline. Our end of the bleachers cheered. Even some of the Basketball Blast fans clapped, and someone from their side yelled, "Nice catch, dude!" Which made Spencer's eyes pop wide, and he started dancing in a little circle. Noah jumped up and down, waving the clipboard.

Even Sam stood up. Noah grabbed her wrist so that at least her arm could jump up and down with him, and she didn't stop him.

Then one voice rose above the roar, clear and bright, like a shiny silver bell: "Great game, Tucker!"

I stopped. Glanced around the gym. It was Emma. She'd come out of the Blast's jail and was standing on the sidelines near midcourt, where Kaley T. was still nose to nose with the ref, whining about Spencer's catch.

Emma beamed her mind-jamming smile on me. Gave me a thumbs-up. "Good luck in the championship!" she called out.

I nodded. And stood there in the middle of the gym—in the middle of the leaping, whooping, group-hugging Artful Dodgers—woozy from pure joy, till somebody slapped me a high-five.

I blinked. Dragged my attention back to earth.

Spencer stood in front of me, bouncing from foot to foot, his high-five still waving in the air.

"I told you this was my lucky vest!" he shouted.

"Yeah." I nodded. "Lucky!"

And before I could turn around again to see if Emma was still watching, Dillon came thundering up. Came thundering up and leaped. Dillon Zawicki. Leaped right at me. It wasn't till he hit me that I realized we were doing a chest bump. It was a chest bump with a Sherman tank.

He chest-bumped the wind out of me. Chest-bumped my T-shirt right into my skin. Chest-bumped me to the floor.

I lay on my back on the cold, hard wood, gasping.

"Got our bulletin board back." He reached down with one enormous ball-throwing hand and pulled me up. "Now we go after the helmet."

☆ LAST PLAYER STANDING ☆

Round I	Semifinals	Final
Backcourt Bombers	Backcourt Bombers	Backcourt Bombers
Nuclear Reactors		
Total Takedown	Beethoven's Blitz	
Beethoven's Blitz		
Basketball Blast	Basketball Blast	Artful Dodgers
Calculators		
Checkmates	Artful Dodgers	
Artful Dodgers		Winner

thirty-six

I stood at the edge of the gym floor, waiting, my heart threatening to pound right through my chest. The Artful Dodgers huddled around me. We were supposed to be warming up, but mostly we were wiping our sweaty palms against our shiny sports shorts.

Talking, laughing clumps of Earhart middle-schoolers and parents had filled the bleachers. The rumble of voices swelled to fill every space in the gym. The gym floor quivered beneath our feet with the noise.

I tried to push my pounding heart back into my chest.

This was it. This was the championship. And just so nobody would forget, Mr. Petrucelli had wheeled in a table and set it up along the sideline at midcourt.

"Our presentation table," he'd said.

He draped it with a slick red tablecloth, and on it, he placed the helmet.

The red and gold batting helmet.

The prize for the Last Player Standing.

He'd gotten the Audiovisual Club to set up the lighting so that two spotlights shone directly on the helmet, and now it sat there, in the center of the table, all by itself, glittering under the hot, bright lights.

Audiovisual Club had stuck around, hanging with Noah. I figured it was because Mr. Petrucelli needed them to turn off the spotlights afterward.

Until I heard the first glimmer of music. It started low, so low I doubt the rumbling herd in the gym even noticed it at first. It grew louder—gradually—till by the time the crowd realized what they were hearing, it had become part of the very air around them.

I blinked in surprise and glanced back at Noah. He nodded and gave me a thumbs-up. So did Audiovisual Club.

Because this was no cheery dodgeball warm-up music. This was darker, with a thundering beat. It was the music from the assembly. The music Noah and Coach Wilder had put together. The tortured superhero music.

The sound swelled. Voices dwindled as the crowd stopped talking and began listening. Then—

BAM!

—the music stopped.

The gym went black.

Silence echoed through the dark.

And when the lights blazed back on, there we were, the Artful Dodgers, lined up on our side of the court, fierce in our snug black caps.

The Backcourt Bombers faced us across the court, eyes wide. Even Wesley looked a little surprised. And maybe impressed.

He recovered quickly, of course. He cut a look at the Sundances.

"What? Was that supposed to scare us?" he said. "Ooooo. I'm just shivering with fear."

And they all laughed like maniacs, like it was the most hysterical thing they'd ever heard. They swaggered and strutted, too, just so everyone would know how completely fearless they were.

But I saw it. For a fraction of a sliver of a nano-second, Wesley Banks had been surprised.

And impressed.

And maybe, in that tiny instant, worried.

Both teams waited behind their end lines. Our hands had to be touching the cool cinder block wall.

I took a deep breath and glanced at our side of the packed bleachers. Mom, Beecher, and Sam's grandpa sat in the front row again. And Emma sat right behind them. On our side. The Artful Dodgers' side. For a second I even thought I saw Caveman. Which was weird. He never left his shop. But it must've been the glare of the spotlights or something, because when I tried to find him again, he wasn't there.

"Both teams ready?" said the ref.

She blew her whistle, and we shot like rockets across the court.

We snatched up dodgeballs. Shoveled them back to our throwers—Owen and Olivia, and me. But mainly Dillon.

Dillon could hold three dodgeballs in his left hand while throwing with his right hand and—BAM, BAM, BAM—pounding the Backcourt Bombers.

He picked two of them off right away.

But a couple of our scoopers went down too. One of them was Martin, who really took one for the team. From the first second of the opening rush, the Bombers had made it clear they were gunning for Owen and Curtis. Trying to take them out for being traitors to the basketball team.

It made zero sense, since Wesley had already cut them from his dodgeball roster. But I guess in Wesley's world, they were still supposed to be loyal and sit in the bleachers and cheer the Bombers on, even though he wouldn't put them on the team.

The Bombers pummeled Owen and Curtis, who did a good job of dodging their throws.

Curtis, one of our catchers, even caught one right at his feet, sending one of their players to jail.

But just as Owen fired one off, Wesley threw. Threw a missile. Threw it right at Owen, who was still off balance and didn't see it coming.

Martin saw. He dove in front of Owen. Dove between Owen and the missile Wesley had just let loose. He tried to catch it and he did get a hand on it. But the ball shot through his arms and slammed into his chest.

"Out!" cried the ref.

Martin nodded and picked himself up off the gym floor.

"That's okay," he said as he trotted toward our jail. "At least Owen's still in there throwing."

While the Bombers were bombing Owen and Curtis, Dillon was able to pick off a couple of their players. I hit one too. Gretchen almost got one—Wesley. Yeah. Gretchen of the woven artistic belts almost hit Wesley Banks.

That's when I remembered that morning at the Atomic Flapjack, when Beecher had pressed his hands together into a little point to demonstrate Wesley's meanness.

Wesley was focused now. Focused on his wedge of mean—Owen and Curtis—and not paying much attention to anything else. And the rest of the team was following their leader.

They were bigger than us (well, except for Dillon). And stronger than us (except Dillon). And faster. And more athletic. And had bigger muscles (except Dillon). And they were filling our jail faster than we were filling theirs.

But we had an advantage too. We could catch them off-guard while they were focused on their wedge of mean.

I ran past Dillon. "Wesley," I said. "Not paying attention."

Dillon nodded. "Yep."

Gym shoes squeaked against the wood floor. Balls thudded against legs, stomachs, cinder block walls. The crowd in the bleachers clapped and cheered, and the sounds echoed through our barn of a gym.

We picked off another Bomber. And another.

And they picked off a couple Artful Dodgers.

Both teams dwindled. The jails filled.

Till suddenly there were six of us: Wesley and the Sundances against me, Dillon, and Spencer.

"Don't worry," Spencer yelled as he darted past. "Think of me as cannon fodder. You guys do your thing. I'll draw all the fire toward me. We can win this."

"You hear that?" Wesley laughed his cold, hard laugh. "Scrawny little loser thinks he's going to win."

Luke laughed too. T.J. let out a feeble "heh heh."

But that game-winning catch against Kaley T. had given Spencer confidence.

"You're going down, Banks," he said, his bony

238

elbows flying all cockeyed, his gangly legs pumping across the floor. "We took out almost your whole team already, and we'll take you out, too."

He dodged and weaved as only Spencer could. Lucky stocking cap bobbing on his head, lucky knitted vest flying behind him, Spencer charged to center court, batted the dead balls back to me and Dillon. He shielded us, running zigzag across the court, drawing fire, as Dillon and I started throwing—*bam, bam, bam*—like a pair of crazed pitching machines.

But I saw Wesley glance at the Sundances, and suddenly all three of them were throwing at Spencer. Trying to pick him off for his trash talk, I guess.

Spencer did a good job of dodging. And Dillon and I tried to cover him with throws. But with three of them pelting him with ball after ball, he couldn't sustain it. He dodged T.J.'s throw. Then Luke's. But Wesley's blindsided him. Slammed him right in the back as he turned, and this time his vest couldn't save him.

So there we were. Two of us against three of them. Dillon and I looked at each other. And nodded. We were outnumbered. But we weren't beaten.

Without Spencer, I had to do double duty: scoop balls to Dillon and fire off shots in between, leaving Dillon free to just throw. I flew around the court, dodging and scooping with such intensity that at some point I lost my snug black hat.

It was a good system. And it worked. For a while.

But then Dillon ran out of balls. I passed one to him and as he grabbed for it, Wesley threw.

The ball came hard and fast. A total line drive.

Dillon turned. His eyes locked onto the ball. He lunged. And as he dove out of the way, the back of his foot came up.

The ball grazed across the heel of his new tennis shoe. Barely. Barely touched him. Didn't even change the direction of the ball.

But it was enough.

"Out!"

I blinked. That was it.

Now it was just me.

thirty-seven

Me . . .

   . . . against Wesley and Luke and T.J.

From the sidelines, Coach Wilder clapped his hands. "You got this," he hollered.

Mrs. Frazee threw a jangly arm in the air. "Remember your performance art!" she called. "Now you have to play all the parts!"

"The little dude," Dillon said as he plodded toward our jail. "We're doing this for the little dude. Sam loves that kid. So do this thing."

Yeah. I caught the gleam of the red and gold helmet under the spotlights. *Let's do this thing.*

I thundered across the gym floor, plucking up balls. Mrs. Frazee was right. I had to play all the parts. I had to scoop and catch and throw. And I couldn't catch the Bombers off-guard, because now their wedge of mean was zeroed in on me, and only me.

Our jail had erupted, cheering, jumping, pumping their fists.

The whole gym was cheering. Screaming, stomping their feet against the bleachers — middle-schoolers, parents, my mom, Sam's grandpa, Emma. Probably more were screaming for the Bombers, screaming for them to finish me off. But the Artful Dodgers side was loud too. The gym walls seemed to swell from the noise. It thundered in my ears till I could barely hear my own hammering heartbeat.

Then one voice cut through the roar: "Do it, Tut! Do it!"

As I fired off a throw, I glanced at the front row. At my goober of a brother, his pillowcase cape tucked into his shirt, his chubby fist swinging in the air.

"Do it!" he yelled again.

Laughter rippled through the bleachers. From people who thought he was cute.

Wesley laughed too. But not because he thought Beecher was cute.

"Yeah, do it, Tut," he yelled across the court at me.

I scooped up another ball, dodged a throw from T.J., and fired.

"Oooo. Nice throw, Tut," yelled Wesley. "Almost got me, Tut."

That was Wesley, focused so hard on his little wedge of mean, he didn't notice what was going on around him.

Because those people sitting close to Beech? The ones who thought he was cute?

They started watching Wesley, and not because they thought he was a superhero. Every time Wesley called me Tut, more people started watching. And cheering.

For me.

I snatched up two balls. Dodged across the floor in Spencer's famous zigzag, watching for my opportunity.

Luke threw. I jumped out of the way. And before I had even landed on both feet again, before Luke could recover, I whipped off a shot. Caught him completely off balance.

Wham!

Hit him in the shin. "Out!" called the ref.

"*Tut!*" yelled the crowd. "*Tut!*" They started slow, then picked up steam, like a freight train. "*Tut! Tut! Tut! TUT!*"

They didn't say it like Wesley did. They didn't say it mean. They said it like . . . a cheer. And not just the Artful Dodgers side of the bleachers. Everybody.

When Wesley first heard them yell "*Tut,*" he thought they were yelling for him. He thought they were on his side, using his words to spur him on. He even lifted his chin toward the crowd in acknowledgment.

That's when he realized they weren't cheering for him.

"*Tut! Tut! Tut! TUT!*" They clapped their hands and stomped their feet in rhythm with the cheer.

I scooped and dodged and scooped in rhythm with the crowd.

I was getting into it now, feeling confident. I *could* do this thing. I scooped up a ball and fired it sidearm at T.J. in one smooth motion.

The ball took flight. It didn't slam into his ankle like a line drive. It rose through the air like a pop fly.

"Catch it!" Wesley yelled at T.J.

T.J. positioned himself. He didn't weave or float around the gym like I always did. He just planted himself under the ball and waited for it to drop.

"*Tut's* going down." Wesley looked me right in the eye. He didn't even bother to throw at me, that's how sure he was. "*Tut's* toast."

T.J. flicked his eyes toward Wesley. Just for a second. Then flicked back to the ball.

"About time too," said Wesley. "Like your little dork of a brother needs a batting helmet."

This time T.J. looked at Wesley. Turned his head and looked right at him. He still held his hands out. But he was looking at Wesley.

The ball dropped. Dropped right through his hands and bounced on the floor.

"Out!" called the ref.

T.J. nodded. He didn't look at the ball or the ref. He kept looking at Wesley. Looked at him as he walked all the way to the Bombers' jail.

And now it was just Wesley. Wesley against me.

He didn't look worried. Not even a little bit. A minute ago, when Dillon had gone down, and it was me facing Wesley and the Sundances all by myself, I'd been worried.

But Wesley had his game face on. Wesley always had his game face on.

And now that game face was mad. Mad at T.J. for dropping the ball. Mad at me probably for just being born.

He snatched up a ball. Charged toward the center line like a bull.

I grabbed a ball too.

As I started to throw, all I could see was Wesley's green dodgeball hurtling toward me, so fast it practically scorched the air. But I still gripped my own ball, and in that moment, that split second before Wesley's ball hit me, I held it up. Held it between Wesley's ball and my face.

Wesley had hurled a bullet, and when it slammed into my dodgeball, it ricocheted. Shot like a rocket straight up in the air, toward the rafters.

At first I was just glad I'd deflected it. But the Artful Dodgers were screaming at me.

"CAAAAATCH IIIIIIT!" One voice echoed above the others. It was Coach Wilder.

I shot a panicked look at him. At his face, bulging and purple, his beefy hands flapping up, up, toward the dodgeball rocketing above me.

I dropped the ball in my hand. Gazed up at the ceiling. Tried to find Wesley's ball in the buzzing gym lights. I finally located the small green dot. I wove across the gym, head back, eyes up, and positioned myself below it. As the dot reached its peak and started to fall, I kept my gaze locked on it, even though the ceiling lights nearly blinded me. The dot became bigger and bigger as it fell.

"TUUUUUUCKEEEEER! JUUUUUUUMP!"

This time it was Noah. His voice was a screech.

I glanced at Wesley just as another ball, red this time, came whizzing toward my feet. I did a little hop dance a nanosecond before the ball would've hit my ankle. It sailed past and slammed into the back wall.

I looked up again, and the green ball dropped against my chest.

What happened next was kind of a blur. But I had it. I had the ball in my arms.

And then, just as I was about to let myself breathe, it squirted back out. Looped right out of my arms.

And with a dull thud of my heart, I knew it was

over. I knew that as soon as the ball dropped, as soon as it touched the floor, I'd be out. The game would be over. The helmet would be Wesley's. And there'd be nothing I could do about it.

But the ball, the green dodgeball, hadn't hit the floor yet.

I dove. Dove at the hard gym floor, my elbows hitting, then my belly. I skidded across the wood, my arms outstretched—

—and caught the ball in both hands.

And before it could pop out again, I rolled to my back and hugged it tight to my chest.

"OOOOOOUUUUUUUT!" shouted the ref. "GAME OVER!"

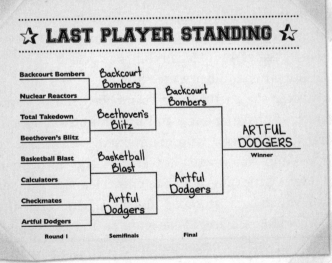

☆ **LAST PLAYER STANDING** ☆

Backcourt Bombers	Backcourt Bombers		
Nuclear Reactors		Backcourt Bombers	
Total Takedown	Beethoven's Blitz		ARTFUL DODGERS
Beethoven's Blitz			Winner
Basketball Blast	Basketball Blast		
Calculators		Artful Dodgers	
Checkmates	Artful Dodgers		
Artful Dodgers			
Round 1	**Semifinals**	**Final**	

thirty-eight

I was wrong about the universe. I owed it an apology. It wasn't working against me. It just needed time to warm up. Probably I caught it off-guard when I decided to get athletic all of a sudden, and for a little while there, it didn't know what to do. Probably it had to recover before it kicked things in gear.

But when it did, it *kicked* things.

After the Artful Dodgers mobbed me at center court, after we spent a full five minutes whooping and jumping in a wild clump that even Dillon got into—and Noah, and Mrs. Frazee, and even Coach Wilder a little bit—after the crowd leaped to its feet and yelled and stomped the bleachers, and after Mom and Beech and Sam's grandpa and Emma and a bunch of Artful Dodger parents stormed the court to cheer and hug us, too, after all that, the gym settled down, and Mr. Petrucelli wheeled his presentation table to center court.

We gathered round, pink-cheeked and out of breath.

The Artful Dodgers stood on one side. Dillon and Sam stood beside their grandpa, who had looped one arm around each of them and looked so proud, I thought for sure his chest would explode right through his neatly pressed work shirt. Beech leaned against me, his pillowcase cape tangled between him and my legs. Mom stood behind us and couldn't stop ruffling our hair, which usually I might not like in public, but now I didn't mind. Noah and Mrs. Frazee pressed in beside us.

The Backcourt Bombers stood opposite. Out of sportsmanship, I guess, although Wesley wasn't looking like much of a sport.

T.J. stood closest to the Artful Dodgers, way away from Wesley. I glanced at him and he met my eyes. He raised his chin at me in a half nod.

I nodded back.

Coach Wilder had brought in his sound system for our pregame music, and now he handed the microphone to Mr. Petrucelli.

"Thank you." Mr. Petrucelli faced the crowd. "As you all know, this dodgeball tournament isn't just the highlight of our annual school carnival. For the students at Earhart Middle, it's the highlight of the entire school year. They each dream of one day being the Last Player Standing, and this year, to make that honor even more special, one of our students, Wesley Banks, out of his love for his school and his respect for athletic competition, has generously purchased a prize with his own money."

Mr. Petrucelli paused to let the crowd clap politely.

"And now here's Wesley," he said, "to present that prize to this year's Last Player Standing—Tucker MacBean."

The crowd cheered.

Wesley shook his head in disgust. He strutted up to the table in his jumbo basketball shoes, grabbed the helmet from the table, and started to shove it at my gut.

But then I guess he realized the whole gym was watching him. He shot a quick glance at all those people. He held up the helmet so everyone could see, flashed a big smile, leaned over, and with a big flourish, placed it on Beecher's head.

Mrs. Stephenson, English teacher and yearbook sponsor, rushed forward with her camera. "We need a shot for the yearbook," she said.

Next thing I knew, Wesley and I were crowded together with Beech, Wesley's hand gripping my shoulder, his other hand patting Beech on top of his helmet.

"Inspirational!" said Mrs. Stephenson.

Her flash exploded in my eyes.

By the time I'd blinked away the spots, Wesley was gone. I guess he could only take so much inspiration.

"Congratulations, Tucker." Mr. Petrucelli stretched out his arm and gave me a serious principal hand-shake, but when he looked at me, it wasn't a serious look at all. He was smiling. Really smiling. Like he wanted to, not because he was the principal and he had to.

Then he did something weird. He turned and nodded at Noah and Mrs. Frazee.

Noah motioned his head toward Audiovisual Club, and I heard the first hint of music. It started low, then grew louder as the gym itself grew darker.

The music swelled to a peak, and in that instant, the video flashed on.

I stared at it. It was our assembly. The video from our assembly. Well, not all of it. Just the last part, the part that had been cut short, the part Earhart Middle hadn't gotten to see.

The part about Beanboy.

Audiovisual Club beamed it onto a screen in the gym.

The crowd had gone still, watching the video, and now I heard gasps. A murmur swept through the bleachers.

"It was him," I heard someone say.

"All those pages in the hallway—it was *him*."

"He's the secret comic book artist."

The crowd cheered.

They knew. Earhart Middle knew. I'd won a (prestigious! national!) contest, and at last they knew.

In the flickering light from the video, I saw Mrs. Frazee smile.

"So it *was* you," I said. "You were the one who taped my Beanboy pages all over the school."

Mrs. Frazee shook her head in surprise. Her earrings clanked against her cheeks.

"It wasn't me. It's the greatest performance art Earhart Middle has ever seen, and I couldn't be more proud." She gave my arm a two-handed proud-art-teacher squeeze. "But it wasn't me."

I blinked. "It wasn't?"

"Nah, she didn't do it." Dillon reached over and gave me a friendly shoulder punch. About punched my shoulder into my chest cavity. "It was me."

Now I *really* blinked. I stood there, my mouth open.

Dillon shrugged. "Sam said I had to. She did all

the copying on Grandpa's Xerox machine at home, the one he uses for farm accounts. But she made me tape them all up because I'm taller."

Sam caught me looking at her through the flickering light and pierced me with a glare, a Don't-Think-I-Was-Doing-You-Any-Big-Favors-'Cause-I-Wasn't-Beanboy glare. She crossed her arms over her army jacket. "I had to do *something* to keep him out of trouble," she said.

I nodded. "I know. But thanks."

She nodded too, and her glare faded. Her arms unclenched just a little. "No problem," she said.

The light fluttered, and the music rose to one last echoing chord. I turned toward the video.

And there on the screen . . .

. . . was a poster. A poster I'd never laid eyes on until that very moment.

The video ended. The music faded. The gym lights blazed on.

The bleachers were abuzz. And even though I couldn't see much, I could hear. Everyone clapped for the video, but then my finely tuned auditory senses picked up bits of conversation:

"He *did* that? Tucker MacBean? Somebody we actually know?"

"He won that contest, and now he's some kind of, I don't know, international comic book artist or something."

H2O Submerged, Episode Ten:

RESURGENCE

Featuring H2O's new sidekick,

BEANBOY

This time, it's personal.

"And he's just walking around our school, like a regular kid."

And as I stood there blinking, trying to regain my vision in the sudden brightness, I thought I saw Caveman.

I figured my eyes were just playing tricks on me again, figured once I could actually see something, Caveman would be gone.

But he wasn't.

I rubbed the glare out of my eyes, and there he was. Caveman.

Standing next to Mr. Petrucelli in the Amelia M. Earhart Middle School gym, his wild black hair fluttering, his Hawaiian shirt stretched over the mounds of his shoulders.

And he had legs. Actual legs. There they were, two tree trunks poking out of a pair of khaki shorts, black hairs bristled up all over them.

"Dude," he said to me. "Couldn't get the actual comic book. Won't be out till summer." He looked kind of sweaty and out of breath. Probably because he'd just said twelve entire words in a row and he wasn't used to that kind of exertion.

"Not a problem," I said. "The poster was—wow."

It really was.

Caveman turned to leave. "Thanks, Mr. P," he said over his shoulder.

Mr. Petrucelli nodded. "Good to see you again, Kevin."

Kevin? I stared at him, at the back of his Hawaiian shirt ambling its way out of the gym. Caveman's name was Kevin?

Mr. Petrucelli thanked everyone for coming, then

rolled his presentation table out of the gym. The crowd clanked its way down the bleachers and trickled out. The Artful Dodgers melted away with their parents. My mom stood off to one side, talking to Sam's grandpa and Coach Wilder and Mrs. Frazee. Beech stayed right by my side, his cape tangled in my legs, just soaking up all the pure happiness of having that helmet on his head.

"Congratulations, Tucker."

A silvery voice echoed through the nearly empty gym.

I looked up and there was Emma, beaming her mind-jamming superpower on me. And even after a few games of dodgeball, even with her hair falling out of her sporty ponytail, she was still the shiniest person in all of Wheaton, all of Kansas, probably all the universe. She'd found my black cap and now she held it in her perfect hand.

"I *thought* the phantom comic book artist was you," she said. "Every time I saw a new page, I wondered. I knew it had to be somebody special."

And then she did something really surprising. She revealed another superpower, a power even more forceful than her mind-jamming shininess.

She put her hands on my shoulders, leaned toward my cheek—

—and kissed it.

And as I stood there, completely paralyzed inside

my own body, the imprint of her kiss burning a warm, toasty hole right through my cheek, she started to put the snug black hat on my head. Then she stopped and pulled it onto her own head instead, right onto her perfect, shiny hair.

"Well, congratulations again," she said.

Then she leaned down and looked under the helmet, looked Beech in the eye.

"You look amazing," she told him. "You're a total superhero."

She kissed Beecher's cheek, too, gave me one last mind-jamming smile, and trotted toward the exit, my cap still on her head, beaming her shininess all over the gym.

Beech stared after her, his hand touching the toasty warm place where she'd kissed him. The helmet fell down over his face, and he pushed it back so he could see her.

"I superhero," he said. "She say I superhero."

I nodded. "You've got the helmet. You're the superhero."

He looked up at me. The helmet wobbled back and forth. "Really?"

"Really," I said. "You, Beecher MacBean, are the greatest superhero I know."

Tucker MacBean's Top Secret Undercover Beanboy Comic Book Page #10:

Caveman restored his favorite
club to its rightful place at
Earhart Middle...

...Dillon found his Art Club project...

...Great-Aunt Bernice found
a whole new way to share
her knitting with the world...